1/10

D0374503

Bismillah.
To my *walaalo*, Safia J.
And my Abo, thank you for everything.

From Somalia, with Love copyright © Frances Lincoln Limited 2008
Text copyright © Na'ima B. Robert 2008

First published in Great Britain in 2008 and in the USA in 2009 by
Frances Lincoln Children's Books, 4 Torriano Mews,
Torriano Avenue, London NW5 2RZ

First paperback edition 2009

www.franceslincoln.com

British Library Cataloguing in Publication Data
available on request

ISBN: 978-1-84507-832-4

Printed in the United Kingdom

1 3 5 7 9 8 6 4 2

From Somalia, with love

Na'ima B. Robert

F

FRANCES LINCOLN
CHILDREN'S BOOKS

Chapter 1

Last weekend Hoyo, my mum, gave me the best news ever and the most shocking news ever. After five long years of looking, waiting, meeting and negotiating, my *habaryero*, my mum's sister, is finally getting married. That is the best news ever.

And then the most shocking news ever: after twelve years of absence, of being missing, Abo, my dad, is finally coming home from Somalia.

It was last Saturday morning that Hoyo got the phone call. Abdullahi, Ahmed and I were sitting in the kitchen, eating hot *anjero* with loads of butter and sugar. Ahmed was entertaining us with another one of his crazy stories when Hoyo came in. As soon as I saw her face, I knew that something major had happened. She had tears in her eyes and the colour had drained from her face.

"That was Abo," she whispered, her lips trembling. "He's coming home…"

And I felt everything around me freeze: silence from the street, steam frozen in mid-air, me, unable to move or think or say anything. Abo? Coming home?

4

Just over a year ago, we had received the news that Abo was still alive. Before that, we all assumed that he had been killed during the fighting in Somalia. So many other families had lost relatives in the war – we thought that we had too. That was until last year when Uncle Yusuf received a letter from his cousin's nephew, telling him that Abo was alive and that he was trying to find us. But I don't think we understood; don't think we thought it was real. We knew about the war, about stolen passports and smuggled visas. But I don't think any of us thought we would really see our father again.

Abdullahi was the first to speak. "Abo's coming home, Hoyo? *Wallahi*? Really?"

Hoyo nodded as the tears began to run down her cheeks. "Haa, haa! He finally found a way to get out, to come to us."

Abdullahi smiled and shook his head. "*Alhamdulillah*! Praise be to Allah! That is fantastic news!" He gave Hoyo a hug and she laughed through her tears.

"*Alhamdulillah*!" she cried. "Allah is Great!"

Then Ahmed went to hug her and, though I was numb with shock, I got up too. She held us all, looking into our faces with new pride, her eyes shining.

"Just wait until he sees what a fine family he has,

5

masha Allah," she said proudly.

★★★

I crept into the boys' room later than night. I couldn't sleep.

"Ahmed," I whispered. "Are you awake?"

"Yeah," came the voice from the mound of covers. He was wide-awake: I could tell from his voice.

"Ahmed, I want to talk to you…" I waited for him to disentangle himself from the sheets and sit up. "What do you think about Abo coming home?"

He sighed and ran his fingers through his mop of tight curls.

"Safia-girl, I don't know… I really don't know what to think."

That was not the answer I had been expecting. "But aren't you pleased he is finally coming over?" I needed Ahmed to make me happy about Hoyo's news, to change my heart from the awful heaviness that I had been carrying all day to something lighter and easier to bear. But he didn't.

"All I know is that things are gonna be different with Abo around."

"What do you mean?" I asked, playing dumb.

"Well, for a start, he hardly knows us and he doesn't know this country – it's gonna be a livin' culture shock for him when he gets here and finds us all westernised and not even speaking proper Somali! You know Muhammad, from Ealing? His old man came home and had a fit when he saw that his kids were all smoking, clubbing and going out with *cadaan* girls… he couldn't cope in the end and went out to the Middle East – but not without beating them all first!"

I laughed because Ahmed laughed, but I wasn't sure whether the last part was a joke.

The heaviness in my heart became worse, like a rock weighing down on my insides. I could feel dread spreading through my veins like the bitterest blood. And I knew then that I would not be getting much sleep that night.

***

It sounded strange to say that my father was coming 'home'. My home was a three-bedroom flat on an estate in Tower Hamlets, in London. His home was somewhere I didn't remember, in faraway Somalia. I'd never really wanted to go there.

For the first eleven years of my life, I had hardly thought about him, to tell you the truth. My family was Hoyo, Abdullahi, Ahmed and my mother's extended family. But hearing that he was still alive, hearing his voice over the phone had changed all that.

Now I had a father, but one I didn't know.

I went over what Hoyo said a thousand times in my head. I let the words roll off my tongue: *Abo is coming home*. So many emotions were fighting inside me: anxiety, nervousness, fear and hope, all at the same time. It took me ages to fall asleep.

***

"Come on, class, settle down... settle *down*!"

I watched my favourite teacher, Miss Davies, hand out a batch of forms to my wild Year 9 class.

She smiled at me briefly as she handed me a creamy white paper. I looked at it: not another school survey! I rolled my eyes at my best friend, Hamida, who was sitting next to me as usual.

She grinned and shrugged her shoulders. "Less time for poetry today – woo hoo!" she whispered.

I stuck my tongue out at her – she knew how much I looked forward to English lessons. I sighed and looked down at the form.

Ethnicity: Somali

I was never sure which box to tick on those ethnicity forms. Sometimes, I was 'Black African', other times I was 'Somali'. On some forms, I was labelled 'British' (because of my passport) and on others I was down as 'Muslim' (because of my religion). Although, for most people, the word 'Somalia' reminded them of war and bloodshed, it held a different meaning for me. I grew up surrounded by the Somali *daqaan* – the food, the clothes, the language, the unspoken rules – and they were a part of me.

Religion: Islam

I couldn't tell anyone what it's like to be a Muslim: it was all I had ever known. It was also a part of me, just like eating and sleeping. I had always been aware of the existence of Allah. I had been learning about the Prophet Muhammad, peace be upon him, since I was knee-high and, while other children had nursery rhymes, my mother recited the Qur'an to get us to sleep.

Praying five times a day, fasting in Ramadhan, going to *duksi* to learn how to read and recite the Qur'an, wearing *hijab*, not eating ham sandwiches – all these things were all second nature to me now. So there you go.

Name: Safia Dirie

Strictly speaking, Dirie was not my surname. Dirie was my grandfather, Awowo's first name but that's the way we Somalis name ourselves: you are 'so-and-so the daughter of so-and-so' and you stay 'daughter of so-and-so', even when you get married. But my mum didn't understand about surnames when she had to fill in birth certificates and NHS registration forms for us: she just put down my Awowo's name as our last name. So that was how she became 'Mrs Dirie' on school letters, even though her name is actually *Nawal bint AbdelQadir*: Nawal daughter of AbdelQadir.

Age: 14 ?

In some ways, I felt a lot older than I was. I always considered myself mature for my age, especially compared with the other kids in my class. My theory was that it was because I had quite a lot of responsibility at home and had to be 'sensible' most of the time. I didn't get the space to behave like a spoilt baby at home – I had to do my bit, especially as the only girl! I remember complaining to Hoyo once about how all my friends got to do absolutely nothing at home and never had to worry about cleaning or looking after younger nephews and nieces. She gave me a funny look then.

"Safia, do you know how easy you have it here compared to back home in Somalia?"

I had heard this speech before.

"By the age of 11, I was cooking meals for the family and, as you know, your auntie was married by the time she was your age!"

Married? At my age? No way! Hoyo took one look at my horrified face and laughed.

"Don't worry, Safia," she giggled, "I'm not planning to marry you off just yet... you still need to learn to make *anjero*!"

At that we both laughed. There was one thing that Hoyo wanted me to have almost more than anything else: a good education.

"With a good education, Safia," she often said to me, "you can do anything, *insha* Allah."

But some of the things the girls talked about in the changing room made my eyes bug out of my head. If Hoyo only knew! The parties, the drinking, the clubbing, the boys – she would have a heart attack. So, although I was more mature than the other girls in some ways, in others I was still a baby. I didn't know anything about guys and going out and, to be honest, I didn't think about it that much. In our school, everyone knew that the Muslim girls who wore the *hijab* were 'straight'. Some were nasty about it and called us 'boring', 'uptight' or worse. Any guy with an atom of sense in his head knew that it wasn't worth chatting us up or asking us out: it was a complete non-starter. Besides, my brother Ahmed always said that a guy who chatted up a girl in *hijab* had no respect and deserved a beating!

So, anyway, fourteen-and-a-half, half responsible young woman, half baby.

"Safia," Hamida hissed, "you've been ages with that form! What are you day dreaming about?"

I smiled at her ruefully and then quickly answered the rest of the questions. Nothing exciting there, just the usual demographic data.

Then Miss Davies was at the head of the class again, looking mildly frazzled. "OK, class, please open your books. Did anyone memorise the poem I gave you for homework last week?"

There was a collective groan.

So far, so predictable.

My classmates were not into poetry at all and there was always a huge outcry when we had to read poetry in class. The other kids really tried their best to spoil it: they read in flat, boring voices, or completely missed the rhythm, or skipped out words or pretended that they don't understand even the simplest metaphor. "But Miss, why's he have to call Juliet a sun when she ain't: she's just a bird!"

Miss Davies was patient though. She didn't give up trying.

I admired her efforts to get Year 9 to appreciate clever similes or interesting metaphors. She had even started introducing modern poets and urban spoken-word artists to the syllabus, anything to get the class to respond.

Benjamin Zephaniah had gone down well the week before, but fourteen-year-olds have short memories. Seven days was enough to erode that small victory so, here we were again, stuck with Stacy Haversham reading...

> *We know who the killers are,*
> *We have watched them strut before us*
> *As proud as sick Mussolinis,*
> *We have watched them strut before us*
> *Compassionless and arrogant,*
> *They paraded before us,*
> *Like angels of death*
> *Protected by the law.*

... as if it was the menu at McDonalds! I could have cried!

At last, the bell, and the pain was over. I was the last to leave the class and I saw Miss Davies sitting at her desk, her head heavy in her hands. She sighed and lifted her head, massaging her temples with her fingers. Then she saw me and a smile lit up her face.

"Safia," she said to me, "you are like an oasis on a desert landscape." She didn't need to explain that simile. I'd often thought of our school as a barren desert.

***

"Coming to mine after school?" I asked Hamida, as we joined the eager home-going crowds outside the school building.

"Sure!" she said, a little breathless as she heaved her schoolbag on to her back.

"Are you smuggling out more Jaqueline Wilsons?" I asked.

Hamida rolled her eyes. "How did you guess?"

"I figured…" I smiled as we walked out of the school gate. Hamida had developed a habit of smuggling reading books since her mum caught her reading the latest Jacqueline Wilson novel about teen pregnancy or something. OK, so it wasn't exactly x-rated but it was hot enough for Hamida's mum to ban her from ever bringing them into the house again.

"But she didn't say I could never *read* them, did she?" Hamida retorted.

Whatever you say, Hamida…

We took our favourite route to my house, through one of the few parks on our side of East London, past row upon row of scruffy grey tower blocks, all depressingly similar.

I thought about my estate: the long-forgotten rubbish in the courtyards, the graffiti on the stairwell, the steaming bins chucked just outside the chute.

None of it surprised me any more. I found myself wondering what Abo would think of our estate, what he would think of the UK. Would he like the fact that there was peace: no warlords, no checkpoints? Or would he miss the sunshine, the friendly faces, the familiar sights and sounds of home? Would he feel proud to have running water all the time and lights that work or would he feel ashamed at the swear words etched into the lift door and the stale smell of last night's pub-closing time?

Well, we would soon find out…

When we got to my block of flats, I punched in the code and pushed open the door to the main hallway. Immediately, Hamida and I both heard someone bounding down the stairwell two steps at a time. A young man's voice echoed through the building, Somali words peppered with 'yeah, man' and 'nah, blood', punctuated by a crazy hyena laugh.

Hamida looked at me. "Ahmed?"

"How did you guess?" I laughed.

And, before we knew it, Ahmed, my crazy brother, had arrived on the ground floor.

His face lit up into a big smile when he saw us and he practically jumped on me, grabbing my neck in a wrestle-hug.

"*Asalaamu alaikum, walaalo!*" he said, as I struggled to get free.

"*Wa alaikum salaam*," I spluttered. "Ahmed, get *off* me!" I finally managed to break away, and then tried to frown at him disapprovingly – but I couldn't quite manage it. It didn't help that Hamida was practically dying of laughter.

"You're crazy, you know that?" I muttered, trying to assess the damage to my *hijab*.

"Yeah, I know, sis, I know," he answered, nodding his head. He turned to Hamida and greeted her briefly, keeping a safe distance. He was always respectful to girls in *hijab* although I suspected that, for him, girls who didn't wear *hijab* were another story.

Ahmed's phone rang again and he answered it, backing away out of the door.

"Hey, Ahmed," I called after him, "is Hoyo home?"

He shook his head. "Nah, she's gone to see Habaryero... catch you later, sis!" And he was gone.

"Your brother is a nutter, you know," said Hamida, shaking her head.

"I know," I replied, smiling fondly at the thought of him, my favourite brother.

***

Up on the tenth floor, I opened the door with my key and stood there, relishing the peace and quiet: in a house with a mum and two older brothers, these

16

precious moments were few and far between.

"So how come your mum's gone to see your aunt?" This was Hamida's second home so she needed no invitation to slip off her school shoes and put her bag by the stairs.

"Oh, didn't I tell you my auntie's getting married?" I got some juice out of the fridge and Hamida grabbed two apples out of the fruit bowl.

"*Bismillah*," she murmured, taking a bite, and then opened her eyes wide. "*Masha Allah*! She waited long enough, didn't she?"

"Yeah," I replied, "not quite out of choice though." Habaryero had wanted to get married for ages and ages and I think some of my family had given up on ever finding someone suitable. And then, all of a sudden, Mr Right shows up!

"Wow, two major events for you then: your dad coming over and your auntie getting married... are you excited?"

"About what?" I pushed open the door to my bedroom and put the drinks down.

Hamida followed me, looking around my tiny bedroom. "About your dad coming, of course," she said, peering at the pieces of paper that covered the lilac paint. I was glad she wasn't looking at me.

"I suppose so," I tried to keep my voice steady. "To be honest, I haven't thought about it that much."

"*Astaghfirullah*," she chanted, wagging her finger at me. "You should know it's *haraam* to lie!" She was teasing me but it was true. I *was* lying. I couldn't stop thinking about my dad coming over. I just didn't want to talk about it, that's all.

"Hmm, you'll talk to me when you're ready," she said, taking her *hijab* off and draping it on the bed next to her. "So, have you written any new stuff lately? I didn't see anything new up on the wall."

It was my turn to look around my tiny room: the single bed hopelessly jammed up against the wall, my window draped in some see-through sari fabric that Hamida's mum had given me ages ago, and my poetry collection plastered over every piece of lilac wall available.

As the only girl, I had my own room and I relished the privilege, even though the room was, literally, hardly big enough to swing a cat. I used my room as my retreat when the rest of the house became too hectic. Fights between Abdullahi and Ahmed (common) would send me scurrying up here, as would getting into trouble with Hoyo (much less common). And, once here, with the door closed, I would write poetry, pouring my feelings out on paper.

Most of my poetry I kept hidden in my bottom drawer, behind all my old clothes. But some of it would find its way up on to my wall, along with all the other poetry I had collected, from Shakespeare to Wordsworth, from Zephaniah to Milligan: all my favourite poems were up on the wall for me to read whenever I liked. My version of boy band posters.

"Actually," I said to Hamida, "there's this one…" I handed her a piece of paper from my drawer. She read it silently, according to my rules: if you want to read my poetry, fine, but don't even think about reading out loud – way too embarassing!

'I didn't see you standing there
Somali-British girl

East African-East Londoner
Council estate wanderer
Fish 'n' chips and banana
Tracksuit and bandana

I didn't see you standing there
Somali-British girl
I didn't see you standing there
Somali-British girl
Somali
British
Girl.'

She nodded her head, smiling. "I like it... especially the bit about the fish 'n' chips and banana – Somalis have banana with everything!"

"Remember the time you tried to eat banana with your curry at home and your dad nearly choked on his food?" I laughed.

"Yeah," she giggled, "he thought I'd gone mental!"

Hamida often teased me about Somali culture and I'd poke fun at her Bengali roots. We both knew all the punchlines but we still found it hilarious. Then I glanced at my watch.

"Hey," I said, jumping up, "it's time to pray. Are you in *wudhu*?" Hamida nodded.

"Just a sec then," I said, "I'll be right back..."

I turned on the tap in the bathroom and looked at my reflection in the mirror above the sink.

Brown girl
Dark hair
Mother's smile
Father's eyes

I wondered what Abo would think of me when he saw me. Would he recognise himself in me, his only daughter? Would he think I was pretty? Would he be proud of me?

As I let the cold water splash on to my hands and

began to wash – hands, mouth, nose, face, arms, head, feet – I tried to wash away that sense of dread I could feel creeping through me again.

By the time I had finished making *wudhu*, I felt better. And after the prayer, while Hamida and I were still sitting on the floor, I felt stronger, ready to face this new challenge, ready to take it in my stride. There were not many days to go. Not many days at all.

***

The rest of the week was a whirl of activity. We had received the news that Abo would be arriving on Saturday afternoon and the news sent Hoyo into a flurry of feverish excitement. The whole house had to be spotless, and *everyone* had to help. Abdullahi and Ahmed grumbled but Hoyo was determined. Every day we went out to Whitechapel to shop for Somali delicacies and the best local produce: the fridge and cupboard had to be full of food. We went up to Shepherd's Bush to shop for new *hijabs*, long skirts for me to replace my usual tracksuits, and have our hands painted with henna. Hoyo sent the boys to have their hair cut, but Ahmed point-blank refused, starting another row with Abdullahi.

By the end of the week, the house shone like new. Fresh linen on the beds, the wooden floor polished to perfection, every room scented with *bukhoor*: we were finally ready to receive our guest.

★★★

In the midst of all the excitement, there was a quiet moment, a period of stillness that stuck in my mind. I came to Hoyo's door to ask her for something and saw her old suitcase on the bed. I stood in the shadow of the doorway and watched as she lifted out a delicate *dira'*, a traditional Somali dress, and held it to her face, breathing in its faint smell. She took out another and another and another, making a pile of translucent jewel colours on the bed. Then she sat down and took a big batch of papers from the inside lining and, as she looked through them, tears began to fall from her eyes.

I felt awkward and suddenly ashamed to have seen her like that. I walked back to my room feeling weird. I had seen a side of Hoyo that I had never seen before: wistful, yearning, vulnerable. I didn't understand. What was the deal with those outfits? And what was written on those papers? Why were they coming out now?

I sat on my bed, holding my knees.

Abo hadn't even arrived yet, but already things had begun to change…

Chapter 2

The day that Abo was due to arrive dawned dark and grey. When my alarm went off for the *Fajr* prayer, I switched it off, thinking it was still night time. It was only when Hoyo came into my room to wake me, warning me that the prayer time was almost over, that I realised it was dark because it was raining.

I made *wudhu* quickly and hurried myself into one of Hoyo's huge prayer gowns before joining her on the silky prayer mat, facing south-east, towards Mecca.

As I listened to Hoyo's beautiful voice reciting the Qur'an, my rushed spirits eased and my mind focused on the day ahead: we would bring Abo home today and a new era would begin.

"*Allahu akbar*!" said Hoyo.

Soon, we were in prostration, our faces to the floor.

"Oh, Allah, *Ar-Rahman*, *Ar-Raheem*, please make everything all right today…"

After prayer, Hoyo took down her favourite copy of the Qur'an and opened it. She began to read, her voice rising and falling with the Arabic words, sometimes long, sometimes short. I recognised the verse: it was the story of the prophet Yusuf, Joseph as they called him at school. I had always loved that story: his strange dream, his brothers' jealousy, his journey to Egypt as a slave, his time in the prison and then his ultimate rise to honour at the end of the story, always patient, still compassionate towards those who had hurt him. Yes, I liked that verse.

"Safia, *kaale*, come," said Hoyo, holding out her hand. I took it and she hauled me up off the floor. My feet always managed to get tangled in those prayer gowns!

"It's time to get ready…" she said, heading up the stairs.

"But Hoyo," I protested, "Abo only arrives in the afternoon!"

She nodded. "I know, Safia, but we have a lot to do. And besides, your uncle Yusuf will be here with the car at ten o'clock to pick us up to go to the airport and I don't want to keep him waiting."

I made a face. No, we did not want to keep Uncle Yusuf waiting. Unlike his namesake, he was not known for his patience and compassion: no way!

I hadn't heard the boys up and about yet and I smiled. Yes! I would be able to use the bathroom before all of them. But I had to be quick and quiet. If just one of them got there before me, I was *finished*: it would be a case of playing the waiting game, showering in lukewarm water and, even worse, cleaning up the mess after they had all finished – ughh!

I quickly grabbed my towel from my room and headed towards the bathroom door. But then I saw Ahmed stumbling out of his room, rubbing his eyes, a towel over *his* shoulders. Before he knew what was happening, I made a dash for it and got in and locked the door, smiling to myself as he banged his fist against it.

"Safia!" he croaked. "Come on, let me in first, please!" Bang, bang.

"Dream on, Ahmed!" I sang as I turned the shower on full blast.

"Safia! Come on! You know I can't survive without my hot shower!" I could just imagine him running his finger through his hair in frustration. But today I would ignore him. I wanted to be ready to meet Abo. I needed all the confidence I could get. And confidence does not come from a cold shower on a rainy day and a messy bathroom to clean up. I got into the shower and the hot water drowned out Ahmed's pleas.

Now, normally, our kitchen is pure madness in the mornings: Hoyo calling us downstairs every five minutes, Abdullahi talking about some household stuff to Hoyo or trying to engage Ahmed and me in some sort of meaningful discussion or burying his head in the paper in frustration, Ahmed making a joke out of everything, texting his 'boys' about the day's plans and me trying to watch what I eat and remember whether I have packed all my school things. It's hot, it's noisy and it's fun.

But on the day Abo was due to arrive, everyone became more subdued, reflective. Even Ahmed kept a low profile.

We had cereal and hot sweet tea because Hoyo didn't want the house to smell of frying when we got back. At about 9:30, the phone rang. I could feel everyone tense up as Abdullahi answered it. Was it bad news?

"It's for you, Safia," he said, handing me the phone. For me?

"Hello?" The receiver was damp with sweat – mine or Abdullahi's?

"*Asalaamu alaikum*, you!" I heard chewing over the phone and relaxed immediately: it was Hamida.

"*Wa alaikum salaam*, you," I smiled. "What's up?"

"What time's your dad arriving?" Her voice was perky as usual and I was grateful for the normality of it all.

"We're leaving at ten to go to the airport. Hoyo doesn't want us to be late."

"Hmm, smart move," she said. "Better you get

there early than him arriving and you not being there. Remember what happened with my Auntie Begum?"

It had been Auntie Begum's first trip to the UK and she could only understand a few words of English. Well, Hamida's disorganised dad had written down the wrong terminal and they hadn't realised until an hour after her aunt was due to arrive. By the time they had found her, she was an emotional wreck: hopping mad and spooked by all the people who stared at her in her bright green sari and couldn't understand what she was saying.

"No, *insha Allah*, Hoyo's not taking any chances," I replied. "She's got Uncle Yusuf to take us."

"You had better be ready then!" she chortled. Hamida knew my family so well! Even my mum had long since stopped treating her like an *ajanabi*, a non-Somali. She always ended up using Somali words when she spoke to her, especially when she was telling us both off!

I heard Hoyo calling me from the kitchen: the dishes weren't washing themselves, apparently.

"Look Hamida, I'd better go, OK? I'll chat to you later…"

"OK, girl, call me later, yeah? *Asalaamu alaikum*."

As I washed the dishes, I thought about Hamida and her dad. Out of his five daughters, she was the rebel, the one most likely to speak her mind. No doubt about it, Hamida was feisty. If she didn't like something, she would say so and no amount of embarrassed 'shushing' on her mum's part would make her shut up: 'a true Bengali social disaster', was what she called herself. And in a community where 'what people will say' is the measure for what is socially acceptable, she was probably right. So, as much as Hamida's mum tried to get her to tone down her opinions and stop reading 'so many nonsense-rubbish books', Hamida just would not conform. "I refuse to live like an Asian stereotype," she would say, sounding just like her dad.

Now, while her dad didn't appreciate the heartache Hamida caused her mum, I could tell that, out of all his daughters, she was his favourite. Maybe it was because she was the spitting image of him; maybe it was because, in her, he could see his own passion and zeal. And although she tried hard to maintain her rebel credentials, I knew that Hamida totally looked up to her dad and copied him in practically everything: from his broad Cockney accent to his left-wing politics. So, if anyone ever wondered where Hamida got her strong opinions from, they didn't need to look far: her father was her role model in everything. She was the son he never had.

I thought of Abo then. Would he be proud of me, like Hamida's dad was proud of her? I thought of my achievements to date: doing OK at school, not getting into any trouble, not hanging out with 'the wrong crowd', wearing *hijab*. Yes, I was sure that would please him: *hijab* to us was a symbol, a symbol of faith and modesty, something every Muslim parent wanted for their daughter. So, even if the other stuff didn't mean much, the fact that I was wearing *hijab* would have to count for something.

I tried to think of something else that Abo would approve of, but couldn't. How could I? I didn't even know him. We would have to wait and see.

***

Uncle Yusuf arrived at ten on the dot. And we were all ready of course, except Ahmed. Don't ask me what he does but that boy always manages to be late, no matter what time he gets ready.

We were all waiting in the car: Uncle Yusuf was making a racket with his horn, Hoyo was apologising, saying '*Sabr, sabr lahow!*' and Abdullahi was huffing and puffing. I could see another argument looming. I just stared out of the window at the estate door, willing Ahmed to come down before Abdullahi lost his rag.

Just as Abdullahi was about to go up and fetch him, the door opened and Ahmed came out, holding

29

his jacket over his head to keep the rain off.

As soon as he got into the car next to me, Abdullahi gave him the obligatory blasting. For once, though, Ahmed didn't retaliate. He just nodded and said, "sorry, man, sorry." I think he had seen Hoyo's face and didn't want to upset her. She hated it when they argued.

"OK, Abdullahi," she said at last, "*isdaya*! He's here now, let's just go!" Then she apologised to Uncle Yusuf again. Uncle Yusuf shot Ahmed a dirty look through the rear view mirror. I felt sorry for the gear stick as he slammed the car into reverse. I shook my head at Ahmed, then squeezed his hand. He squeezed it back.

★★★

Ahmed and Abdullahi had fought the previous night too.

"Where have you been?" Abdullahi hadn't waited for Ahmed to take off his shoes before the interrogation began. It was nine o'clock and we had been expecting him home by seven to eat dinner with us. Hoyo had gone over to her friend's place in a neighbouring estate, leaving me to finish off my homework. But when Ahmed came in, I knew that there was not much chance of that happening.

"None of your business, man," Ahmed mumbled as he pushed past his older brother on his way up the stairs. But Abdullahi grabbed his arm and swung him round.

"I asked you a question!" he barked. "Where have you been?"

Ahmed, a bit unsteady on his feet, looked up into his face and I could see the battle going on in his mind: defy or deny?

"Nowhere, man, I was at college," he said at last, pulling his arm from Abdullahi's grip.

"College?" Abdullahi sneered, looking at Ahmed's empty hands and messed-up hair. "No books, no homework, no studies? What kind of college is this?"

"Ah, leave it off, man," Ahmed waved his hand dismissively. "Don't try your detective work on me, OK? You ain't my dad, you ain't Hoyo, so just keep out of my life, yeah?"

My heart, my stomach, both of them were in knots. I couldn't bear to see my brothers argue, I couldn't stand Abdullahi's cruel words, I couldn't stand Ahmed's ugly voice. I squeezed my eyes shut and prayed for them to stop: for the phone to ring, for Hoyo to come home, anything to stop them going at each other.

But they kept on and on, neither of them willing to back down.

"You think you're a big man, yeah?" shouted Ahmed finally, his face contorted with rage, his arms out to his sides, ready to take Abdullahi on. "You think you're a big man? You're nothin', yeah, nothin' to me!"

"Don't you come in here with your *gedoboy* filth, Ahmed!" Abdullahi was furious and the veins stood out on his forehead. "*Wallahi*, when Abo gets here, he'll beat some sense into you for sure! You're a waste of space, Ahmed! A loser! You hear me? A loser!"

My heart was breaking as I watched Ahmed's face. All the ghetto fire was gone and there he was, a seventeen-year-old Somali boy, trying to get his GCSEs for the second time.

Just then, the *adhan* alarm clock rang out: it was time for *Isha*, the night prayer.

"*Astaghfirullah*," Abdullahi muttered, shaking his head. He pushed his feet into a pair of slippers and left to go the mosque, slamming the door behind him.

Then I could breathe.

I went into the kitchen and found Ahmed leaning against the counter, a glass of water in one hand and his mobile phone in the other. He was trying to send a text – but his hands were shaking so much that he gave up and threw it on to the counter beside him. He wouldn't look at me and I felt awkward, not knowing what to say.

"Ahmed..?" I whispered finally. He looked at me

then, and that mischievous smile came back for a moment.

"Ah, Safia-girl," he said, "don't worry about it, man. It's nothing. Don't worry about old Abdullahi – I can handle him."

I plucked up courage. "But where were you, Ahmed? We were waiting for you…"

"Had some stuff to sort out, *innit*?"

"What, college stuff?"

"Yeah, Safia, college stuff." He saw my doubtful look. "Don't *worry*," he crooned, "trust me, yeah?"

I nodded. I wanted so much to believe him.

"Now look," he said, sitting me down. "You're a good girl, Safia, I want you to stay that way, yeah? No fooling around, OK? You listen to Hoyo and Abdullahi."

"But *you* don't…" I interrupted but he put his finger to his lips.

"Me is me and you is you, OK? We are not the same – you ain't gonna be a loser like me…"

"Oh, Ahmed, I'm sure Abdullahi didn't mean that…" But again he waved his hand.

"It doesn't matter, man, it doesn't matter. All I know is Abo is coming and he'll be expecting certain things. So don't you go disappointing him, or Hoyo. Stay sweet, Safia-girl, stay sweet…" And then he was off, ready to send that text message.

I sat in the kitchen, my arms around my knees, waiting for Hoyo to come home. A poem beat its way into my head.

Fine words, my brother, fine words
Good advice
Keep it nice
Slice of life
Keep it clean
Keep away
Keep the dream
Keep your name
Stay the same
Stay the course
Don't use force
Don't give in
Just stay in
Just be strong
Don't go wrong...
Fine words, my brother,
Fine
Fine
Words.

I drew a ragged breath as I came back to the present.

The drive from East London to West London was

long and slow. The drizzle didn't help the situation. Uncle Yusuf tried his best to stay out of the Saturday morning traffic as we crossed the River Thames but even he couldn't avoid some of the worst bits.

Hoyo turned on the radio to ease the tension in the car. The drone of the radio, the slow-moving traffic and the sound of the rain on the window made my head heavy. I shifted into a more comfortable position…

★★★

"Safia, Safia!" I could hear Hoyo's voice from far away. "Wake up, Safia, we're here!"

It was only then that I realised where we were. We were outside the Heathrow Arrivals Hall and Uncle Yusuf was negotiating a tight parking spot. I had missed the whole journey!

"Come on, sleepy head," Ahmed chuckled, "your snores were killing us!"

Even Uncle Yusuf laughed at that one while I hurriedly wiped my face and smoothed my *hijab*: shame!

When we reached the arrival hall, Uncle Yusuf went to look at the monitor. Abo's plane had landed fifteen minutes ago.

"*Kaale*," called Hoyo, marching ahead, clutching

her handbag. "Come on!"

By the time we had reached the crowd of people waiting for their relatives and friends, we were out of breath and panting.

I scanned the crowd as my heart thumped hard in my chest. Somali men were coming out of the customs area every minute, most of them with woven plastic bags and strange-looking packages. How would we know which one was Abo? Would Hoyo recognise him? Would Abdullahi? I saw a short man with glasses holding a large blue suitcase: was that Abo? But he turned to speak to a little girl who was holding his hand – no, it wasn't him.

I looked at every Somali man, searching for something familiar, a look, a smile.

Then a tall, dark man in a grey suit came walking through the doors. On his head, he wore the *koofiyet* that Somali men often wear. In his hands, he held a pair of battered suitcases. He frowned as he looked across at the sea of unfamiliar faces. And then his eyes met mine and something changed in his face – and I knew immediately that it was him. I felt heat flood my cheeks and a thousand butterflies danced inside me. Abo?

"There he is!" I heard Hoyo cry out.

At the sound of her voice, Abo turned away from me and towards the sound of her voice. He saw her and his face broke into a smile. He began walking, faster and faster, until he stood in front of her. Tenderly, he took her hands. I watched Hoyo as she gazed into his face, tears rolling down her cheeks. Finally, she broke away from him and held out her arms to us, Abdullahi, Ahmed and I. It was only then that they could embrace, holding all of us together.

"*Masha Allah, masha Allah,*" Abo kept saying, over and over again. "This good thing is as God intended." And, for that moment, squashed between my brothers, my mother and my father, I felt completely safe.

Chapter 3

After the emotional meltdown at the airport, Abo became very subdued. He hardly spoke as we drove home. He answered Uncle Yusuf's questions about Mogadishu, but I could tell from his voice that his mind was somewhere else. He stared out of the window at the tall buildings that rose on either side of the road, at the massive billboards, at the rows of shops whose windows glowed welcomingly, offering us things we could never afford. And there was the rain. It didn't stop, coming down from a grey sky in a miserable drizzle.

But if Abo was uncomfortable, if he was wondering what on earth he was doing here, that all changed when we reached Shepherds Bush. Here, there were Somalis everywhere: tall, broad Somali women doing their shopping in their brightly-coloured *jilbabs*, phoneshops selling blankets and *mahlabiyyah* oil, *xalaal* meat being sold, lanky old men wearing crumpled suits, their beards stained orange with henna, sitting in Somali coffee houses. I could see Abo start to relax.

And if Shepherds Bush made Abo relax, arriving at my grandparents' terrace house must have been like coming home.

Uncle Yusuf knocked on the door and smiled at Abo. Then the door swung open and there was my Awowo, with a bigger smile on his face than I had ever seen, his arms open wide, ready to embrace my father. My other uncles, aunts and cousins crowded the narrow passageway behind him, all eager to see their long-lost son-in-law.

"*Asalaamu alaikum, yaa* Hassan!" cried Awowo and the two of them shook hands and embraced, Awowo thumping Abo on the back. Then my grandmother stepped forward, beaming.

"*WarHassano*!" she said in her singsong voice. Abo took her hand and kissed it, our way of showing respect to someone older. The rest of the family cheered and shouted out greetings, welcoming Abo back, inviting him inside, giving *salaams* and congratulations to Hoyo and the rest of us.

The house was packed full of family: my Awowo, Ayeyo, my aunts, uncles and all our cousins. In all, about forty bodies were crammed into the four-bedroom house. Abo, Abdullahi and the men of the family all went into the living room while Ahmed went upstairs with Faisel, one of my cousins. I could hear my uncles' voices rising above each other.

Most of them hadn't seen Abo for over ten years, and I could tell from their beaming faces and firm handshakes how much they had missed him.

No sooner had Abo been pulled into the living room by the men, than we were dragged down the narrow corridor to the kitchen, where Hoyo's mum and her sisters were putting the finishing touches to the dinner. The kitchen was like a furnace and there was steam everywhere. Ayeyo wiped her forehead with a corner of her scarf.

"*Asalaamu alaikum, Hoyo,*" said my mum, taking Ayeyo's hand and kissing it.

Ayeyo did the same. Then Ayeyo took Hoyo in her arms and rocked her to and fro, praising Allah for my father's safe return.

"*Alhamdulillah, yaa Nawal*! My daughter! What a blessing for you: Hassan safely back with you and the children. *Allahu akbar, wallahi,* this is a great day!"

Then she turned to me and put her hands up in the air. "Allah! Even more beautiful than the last time I saw you, *masha Allah,* Safia!" I kissed her hands and she kissed mine before turning back to the onions that sizzled on the stove. Then she began talking a mile a minute about everything: Abo's return, the food, the guests, the state of the kitchen...

I had a peek inside some of the massive pots that were perched precariously on the tiny stove top. My mouth watered as I smelt the delicious smells of raisin fried rice, fried steak and vegetable rice.

Feeling brave, I dipped my hand into the biggest pot and took out some rice and meat with my fingertips, right hand of course!

"'*Eeb, yaa* Safia!" my grandmother screeched, knocking my hand with her wooden spoon. But it was too late: I had already put the delicious cumin-flavoured rice in my mouth.

"Sorry, Grandma," I said with my mouth full, "your food is just too delicious to resist, *wallahi*."

She smiled and clucked disapprovingly. "Stop it now!" she said as she kissed me again.

"Now," she said, folding her arms over her chest, "have you been to see your Habaryero yet?"

Habaryero! Of course! In all the excitement about Abo's arrival and everything else, I had completely forgotten that I had not even seen my aunt since the announcement of her wedding plans.

Excusing myself, I rushed out of the kitchen. As I passed the living room, I could hear a strange chanting in Somali. I couldn't make out the words, just the regular rhythm and repeated sounds.

"What are they up to?" I wondered. But I didn't stop. I went upstairs, stopping briefly to say *salaams* to various aunties and uncles and a quick 'what's up?' to some of my cousins. There were people in every single room, so it took me a while to get to the third floor where Habaryero has stayed for all her single life.

When I got to the door, I knocked and heard Habaryero's voice call out, "*Soogal*!"

I opened the door and saw my mother's youngest sister, my Habaryero, sitting on her bed getting her hair plaited, surrounded by a whole group of my female cousins: Suad sat on the floor with her sisters, Halimo and Hoda, Fadumo leaned against Habaryero's desk, Aisha was trying on some of Habaryero's jewellery, turning from side to side in front of the mirror.

I hadn't seen my cousins for ages and, after giving *salaams* and kisses all round, I perched on the side of the desk, eager to hear all the latest news.

Of course, the main topic of conversation was Habaryero's wedding.

"So, Naima, what are you going to wear?" Aisha put Habaryero's jewellery back in the box and turned to her. "I think you would look wicked in this white wedding dress I saw down Selfridges last weekend. *Nayaa*, it was *hot*, *walaalo*!"

"No, Aisha," answered Habaryero, turning her head so that Asma could start on another plait. "I thought about getting a wedding dress from here *laakinse* I think I'm going to wear one of those new *dira'* that have just come in from Dubai."

42

I thought Habaryero would look gorgeous in a dira', a semi-transparent one with sequins and a heavily embroidered underskirt, but Aisha wrinkled up her nose.

"*Dira'*?" she squealed. "Boring! Every downtown *xalimo* wears a *dira'*. That's dry, man! Don't you want to be different?"

"For real," added Suad, "dem *dira'* are so out of date! I wouldn't be caught dead in one, *nayaa*, no way!"

"Shut your mouth!" retorted Hoda, snapping her fingers in her sister's face. "What do you know about style anyway? I swear, sometimes I have to wear shades coz of the amount of bling you've got on!"

"*Wallahi*, that's so true," Fadumo added. "It's like some Somalis wanna deny their roots, forget where they came from. Weddings these days are all about the big white dress, diamond rings and cutting the cake. A girl can't even wear dira' without getting cussed…"

Aisha flicked her hair away from her face and turned to Habaryero. "I suppose you'll be getting henna as well, eh?"

"And what's wrong with henna, *ha*?" Fadumo and Hoda turned on Aisha and Suad and a heated argument began between the pro-Somali lot and the break-with-tradition camp. I just looked at all of them, laughing at how different they were, and how alike at the same time. But I wasn't fazed by the hot exchange: the women in my family had big mouths, for sure.

"Oh, shut up, you lot!" laughed Habaryero, kicking Suad playfully. "Whose wedding is this anyway?"

We all laughed then and I seized the chance to ask the question that everyone else already knew the answer to. "Habaryero, you haven't even told me: who is the lucky guy? What's he like?"

Habaryero put her head back as Asma started a new row of plaits and a dreamy look came into her eyes.

"Well..." said Habaryero at last, "he's Somali..."

"Yeees..?" we all said together.

"He's from Holland..."

"Yeees...?"

"He's an accountant..."

"Yeees...?"

"And *nayaa*, he's fine, *masha Allah!*"

We all started whooping and cheering and my cousins began teasing her, about her dress, about her henna, about her wedding night. Habaryero blushed and tried to get us to stop but I could see she was enjoying it anyway.

Somehow or other, I got to the bottom of Habaryero's wedding story. Habaryero had met a Somali lady at the school where she was working and this lady had a brother. It turned out the brother was looking for a wife and so he got his sister on the case for him. After working with my auntie for about 6 months, the lady, whose name was Rahma, thought that she would make a good match for her brother. So she called him, he called her, he called my Awowo, Awowo called Habaryero, the guy came over from Holland, they had a meeting, she accepted his proposal and they set a date – next month!

Habaryero's husband-to-be had already sent the traditional gift of gold to Habaryero's family and she brought it out to show us.

Even Aisha and Suad had to admit that the 24-carat gold jewellery that Habaryero held in her hands was gorgeous. The gold was nothing like the gold I had seen in Asian jewellery shops – it didn't have that bright yellow glitter and the intricate designs. This was a warm, almost coppery colour – Arab gold. The designs were bold yet simple and looked stunning against Habaryero's caramel skin.

I was *so* happy for her. Habaryero had been single so long (in Somali terms, that is!) that I think a lot of people in the family had given up on her ever finding someone suitable. Sure, there had been guys who had been interested, but Habaryero wasn't about to settle for just *anyone!* If you ask me, I think she was biding her time. She had always wanted to finish her education, get a job, find herself, that sort of thing.

And now, she had found him Mr Right. I wondered whether I would know the right man for me when the time came.

Then everyone turned to me.

"*Masha Allah*," Habaryero smiled, "your Abo's come from Somalia, after all these years? *Alhamdulillah*, you must be very pleased…"

I smiled and nodded, a lump in my throat, thinking of holding my mother, father and brothers at the airport.

My cousins all murmured about how happy I must be, how amazing it was that he had survived the war. But I didn't miss the raised eyebrows and the look that passed between Aisha and Suad. Suad's dad was the one Ahmed had told me about, the one who had come from Somalia to find his kids *ajanib* through and through. I tried to catch Suad's eye, but she didn't look at me. I could feel the bad feeling start to grow again in the pit of my stomach.

"Hey, has anyone seen Firdous lately?" I asked, changing the subject. "I haven't seen her for ages!"

Again, I saw a look pass between my cousins. I knew why I was not part of the silent communication. Not only was I younger than most of them, but living in East London meant that I didn't see my cousins as often as they saw each other. Not only that, Hoyo wasn't too keen on me going to West London to spend

46

time with them. She never said why but I had heard her muttering about bad influences so I never pushed it. Anyway, Hoyo and I were tight, always had been, so our weekends were quite busy anyway. And I had Hamida too. That had always been more than enough. But now, I felt a pang of regret, a surge of envy for their comfortable closeness, their shared conversations and their secret looks. I felt left out of the loop.

So what was the deal with my other fourteen-year-old cousin, Firdous?

"*Walaalo*, you know Firdous is staying with Auntie Iman now?"

"Huh?" I couldn't hide my surprise. "Why's that? She was staying with Uncle Ismaeel and his family – what happened?"

Another look.

Firdous's parents had split up when she was still in nappies and her mum was in Holland, her dad in Canada. She and her sisters had been staying with different relatives but I had thought that Uncle Ismaeel's house was her home. I couldn't imagine why she would have left there – and to stay with Auntie Iman? The one the kids secretly nicknamed 'Witch of the Ogaden'? It didn't make sense…

Just then, the door opened and everyone turned to see who it was this time.

She stood there at the door for a moment, poised,

taking in everyone's stares. She wore tight-fitting black trousers with a strappy white top that showed every inch of her petite frame. Her blond-streaked hair was straight and smooth, curving over one eye then into a sleek ponytail. Heavy gold earrings hung from her ears and she had rings on every one of her fingers. She looked at everyone steadily, her plucked eyebrows arched, her glossy lips in a half smile.

It was Firdous.

"*Iskawaran, walaalo!*" she said at last, grabbing Suad and hugging her. "What's up, man? Whatcha all starin' at?" That broke the tension and, all of a sudden, everyone was all smiles. Everyone started laughing, talking again. Only Habaryero was silent, looking at Firdous with a worried expression on her face.

I had to fight not to stare, not to let my mouth hang open like an idiot. The last time I saw Firdous, she was on her way home from school: *hijab*, loose grey trousers, blazer, face scrubbed clean, a regular Somali girl like me. But now? She looked completely different: older, sophisticated, more self-assured, more knowing – everything I was not.

Suddenly, I felt small and plain in my pale pink *hijab* and denim skirt. I knew that, even without my loose-fitting clothes, I would never look as good as Firdous did. And I was jealous.

I bit my lip and looked down at the books on

Habaryero's desk. Among her Qur'an and Islamic books, I spotted a few glossy magazines, her 'guilty pleasures', as she called them, and her collection of books from her school days. I was just about to pull one out when I felt a hand on my shoulder.

I spun round to see Firdous smiling at me. She was so close I could see the tiny nose ring in her left nostril and smell her perfume, heavy and cloying.

"*Nayaa*, Safia, long time no see, *ha*?" She hugged me and laughed when I fumbled with my words.

"Umm, yeah… uh, too long," I said. "So, what have you been up to? I heard you're staying with Auntie Iman now? How's that going?"

Firdous raised an eyebrow and popped her gum. "Yeah, well, you know what *adults* are like!" She said that as if she and I were partners in this great conspiracy, this teen rebellion, and I felt grateful for her attention, as if I too could someday be so beautiful that heads turn, that I too could have that sophistication. Strange: I had never wanted it before that day.

"We should hang out some time, you and I," she continued, brushing something off my jumper. "We could go shopping, catch a movie or just hang out."

I swallowed hard and nodded, imagining asking Hoyo if I could go to the mall with Firdous to

49

'hang out'.

"Yeah, that would be cool, really cool." I listened to myself sounding like a complete idiot. But I wanted her to think that I wasn't boring-Safia-Dirie-with-no-life.

So I gave her our house number and she wrote down her mobile number for me. I stuffed it into my bag and smiled at her.

"Make sure you call me, yeah?" she said, turning to me as she walked out of the room.

Habaryero called after her. "Are you going to help Hoyo in the kitchen, Firdous?"

Firdous smiled that lazy half smile. "Nah, I think I'll go chill with Ahmed and Faisel. I want to see my favourite footballer in action: Ronaldo rocks!"

And she was gone.

Habaryero opened her mouth to say something and then thought better of it. I knew what she wanted to say. Ayeyo didn't like us girls spending too much time with the boys and their friends. "That's how problems start," she always said.

As soon as Firdous left, everyone went back to their conversation. But I saw the looks that followed her, I saw the sly whispers. I seethed inside. Why did they have to be so two-faced? Whatever beef they had with Firdous, they didn't have the right to gossip about her. I felt even more apart from them then but this time, I was glad they didn't include me. If there's one thing I hate, it's gossip.

As I started talking to Habaryero again, I wondered to myself what Firdous was really up to, why she was staying with Auntie Iman. And I realised then that she never answered my question.

The meal that night was wonderful, Ayeyo had really outdone herself. As usual, we all sat on the floor around huge trays, passing each other bananas, salad and glasses of water. We ate and ate until we couldn't eat anymore and had to unzip, unbutton and roll down the *gogorat* to make space for our full bellies. We left around midnight, tired but happy. We rode home in a comfortable silence, and it was only when Hoyo shook me to wake me that I realised I had slept through the journey again.

Chapter 4

The first few weeks with Abo home passed in a blur. Everything was different but somehow the same. Abo and Abdullahi would leave early to pray *Fajr* at the mosque which meant that Hoyo and I still prayed together, in our huge prayer gowns, on the glossy smooth prayer mat. We still sat for a while afterwards, Hoyo reciting verses she had learnt when she was a little girl, practising new ones she was learning in her Qur'an class at the mosque. So, in that way, our mornings were the same.

But, too soon, Hoyo would be up and in the kitchen. Now she cooked breakfast every day and there were no more rushed bowls of cereal washed down with juice. Abo was home: things had to be done properly.

In fact, one of the things I remember about those early days is the food. Hoyo made every kind of Somali dish, some I was used to and quite a few I hadn't tried before. It was as if she was determined to make up for lost time and feed Abo every dish she had wanted to cook for the last twelve years. Of course, we weren't complaining!

"Hey, man!" Ahmed would laugh, "Hoyo's food's been giving me a serious pot belly y'know!" – but that didn't stop him eating it! More than once, I came home to find him and his friends in the kitchen, eating Abo and Hoyo's lunch leftovers straight from the pot.

But there were other changes too. Hoyo began putting henna on the tips of her fingers, dark henna that stained the skin burgundy-black and the nails a deep red. Once a week, she would get fresh henna patterns from the lady on the fifth floor.

Hoyo also started wearing her wedding gold again and a new dira' every day: I hadn't even known she owned so many! White, soft grey, black with red starburst patterns, purple with silver swirls, orange with green tie-dye... she had a whole rainbow collection I had never seen before.

Once, Habaryero came over and teased Hoyo: "You're just like an *aroosa* now, *masha Allah*!"

And it was true: although I had never seen Hoyo work so hard, I had never seen her look so radiant.

I saw the way Abo smiled at her when she brought him his food, the melting, tender way she looked at him when he would say, "Remember that day, back in Somalia...?" and they would start another conversation without me, one I couldn't understand. More than once, I had come downstairs in the night to

53

get a drink of water and found them, sitting on the floor in the kitchen, drinking tea, talking quietly.

And while I was happy for Hoyo, I felt cut off by her happiness, left out because I didn't feel it too.

To be honest, I think Abdullahi was the only one out of us kids who was really happy to have Abo home. Abdullahi had been ten years old when we left Somalia so he remembered Abo. His Somali was better than ours and he knew more about the history, the culture, our family back in Mogadishu. So he and Abo had lots to talk about.

"But Abo," he would say, "everyone knows that it was the Ishaqs who sold us out to the Italians in 1950 – if it wasn't for them, Somalia would never have been colonised."

"Well, yes, that's true," Abo would answer, stroking his beard. "But you have to remember that the British also had their eye on Somalia – if it wasn't for the Ishaqs, we'd be eating fish and chips instead of *baasto*!" They both enjoyed that one.

I could tell Abo was an intelligent man – he seemed to know so much about Somalia, politics and history. At first, I tried to appear interested, tried to keep up. But they never included me. So, after a while, I stopped trying. Neither of them noticed. They went to the mosque together to pray and Abdullahi took Abo down to the local Somali shops and introduced him to the older men there. Abdullahi would go with Abo when the other men invited him. I didn't know what it was they wanted Abo to do but once I heard Uncle Yusuf telling Abdullahi: "Your father was one of the best of our generation, one of the very best!" And, as the days became weeks, I saw them develop a bond. I could see that Abo was proud of his eldest son and that Abdullahi was pleased to have his father back again.

This was not the case with Ahmed. I could see straight away that Abo and Ahmed were not going to hit it off. For a start, Ahmed had no time for Abo. He started leaving the house straight after breakfast and coming home late. When he was around, he was silent, withdrawn, and gave one word answers to all our questions. While Abdullahi was full of curiosity, full of questions, Ahmed would roll his eyes and laugh, an empty, harsh laugh, nothing like the laughter I loved to hear. Soon he would be on his phone and go up to his room, leaving Abdullahi and Abo to continue their conversation.

Then I noticed that, every time Ahmed came into the room, Abo would frown, a look of irritation on his face. He criticised everything about Ahmed: his hairstyle, his clothes, his 'gutter Somali'. I cringed inside. I didn't want him to look at Ahmed that way, I didn't want him to start behaving like Suad's dad.

So I would always try to draw Ahmed into the conversation, even if I hadn't been part of it, even if I hardly understood what they were talking about.

"Nah, little sis," he would always say, and then he'd leave the room. Abo's eyes would follow him, a line etched between his brows.

Whenever I prayed, I asked Allah to please make us all get along.

★★★

"So, what is it like, having your dad home?"

Hamida was perched on my bed, sticking a henna transfer on her arm. "Mum says that it's cheating but I don't care," she had said earlier. "I'm not about to sit still, wrapped up like a mummy for hours." She patted her arm to make sure the transfer was stuck on then turned to me.

"Well?" she said, jutting out her chin, "what's it like?"

I twisted my hands in my lap. "Well," I began, "it's weird. On the one hand, it's nice because it feels like we are a 'normal' family now: mum, dad, kids, etc. On the other hand, I hadn't minded it the way it was, you know? I mean, we all got along and Hoyo and I, we were cool, we were really close, you know that."

Hamida nodded. "And now you feel shut out,

is that it?"

"That is *so* it!" I couldn't believe that she had seen that so quickly. "It's like, now that Abo's here, her life is complete. But then what does that say about how she felt when it was just us?" I shook my head. "It's nice that Abo and Abdullahi get along – I'm really happy about that. Boys need their fathers, don't they?"

"But girls need their dads too, you know," Hamida said softly. I looked at her and saw the question in her eyes. I looked down at my hands: my father's hands.

"Well, "I said at last, "maybe not all of us do. And maybe not all dads are that into daughters…"

"What about *your* dad?" Hamida, the future psychologist, was pushing me. We had an unspoken rule: don't push Safia to open up because she won't. Keep it light-hearted and we'll be OK. Now she was trying to do an Oprah on me. But I wasn't about to go there – some things are better left unsaid… or written down.

"I don't know about my dad," I said finally, "he doesn't say that much to me anyway. I suppose he doesn't know what to say. I mean, he'll ask me how I am and if I can bring him some tea or more salt or whatever, but nothing deeper than that…"

I didn't tell Hamida that I wished my dad did talk to me, like he spoke to Abdullahi, asking his opinion, asking him to translate, telling him about Somalia.

57

To me he would say things like, "Safia! Do you know who Siad Barre was?"

I would shake my head. "No, Abo."

"Ah, just what I thought. The children of today know nothing about our history!"

"Never mind, Abo," Abdullahi would say, grinning at me, "as long as she can make *baasto iyo hilib*, she'll be all right!" Then they both roared with laughter.

But he never did explain who Siad Barre was. I guess Abo didn't think I would have anything worth saying, young as I was and a girl as well. As long as I brought him cold water with ice and black tea with four sugars, I was OK as far as he was concerned.

But I didn't mind, really. I wasn't that bothered. At least, that was what I told myself every time I went up to my room, tired of being invisible for yet another evening.

"You know what though?" I said at last. "It's Ahmed I'm worried about."

"Ahmed?" Hamida's eyebrows shot up. "Why?"

"Cos he's just not into this new set-up, he won't even give it a chance." All my worries for Ahmed starting pouring out. "I've seen the way he looks at Abo, the way he watches him when he's eating. It's like he can't stand him. When Abo speaks to him in Somali, he won't look him in the eye and he deliberately answers in English or speaks such broken

Somali that Abo just gives up. He won't discuss anything with him. It's like they have nothing in common and Ahmed won't even make an effort. He's even stopped talking to me..." My voice faltered. Ahmed was closer to me than anyone else in the family. What was happening if he felt he couldn't even talk to me?

Hamida nodded slowly. "Hmm, sounds like the return of the old man has mashed things up a bit. What about your mum, what does she make of it all?"

"Hoyo? She's over the moon!" I couldn't keep an edge of bitterness out of my voice. Hoyo was happy and we were miserable – was this the way things were meant to be?

"It's like they're on their second honeymoon or something! Except that she's always cooking, always cleaning the house, cleaning up after Abo – she won't let him touch a thing in the kitchen, she says it's *'eeb*. I just don't get it..."

"I know!" answered Hamida. "If I ever get married, my husband had better know more than how to boil an egg!"

I laughed then because I knew that Hamida had *burnt* a boiled egg more than once: she was a total disaster in the kitchen!

"But Hoyo doesn't seem to mind, Hamida! She's quite happy to cook and clean for him and treat him like royalty! Me? I would be expecting him to make it up to me for all the years I spent on my own raising his children!"

I could see Hamida was impressed: this kind of talk was suitably rebellious and I felt surprised at myself, surprised and a little pleased: so Safia Dirie did have some fire in her after all, *ha*!

But fire was the last thing on my mind later on that night. Ahmed came home late, really late. I was on my way downstairs to get some water when I heard a key in the door. I looked at my watch: one o'clock in the morning. In the semi-darkness, I could just make out Ahmed's curls and the hunch of his leather jacket. He was breathing hard, trying to avoid the creaky floorboard next to the stairs. I held my breath.

Why was he home so late? Where had he been?

Just then, the kitchen door burst open and there was Abo, his tall frame filling the narrow doorway, anger all over his face.

The light from the kitchen flooded the hall and Ahmed was caught like a rabbit in the headlights. His eyes were red and his clothes tousled. He seemed to be having trouble staying upright and a strange smell drifted up the stairs towards me.

Oh, Ahmed, Ahmed, what have you been doing?

Abo didn't waste any time. In a few steps, he was right in front of Ahmed. He grabbed him by the collar and I saw the look of disgust on his face as he too smelt the strange smell.

"Where have you been?" he shouted, his face close to Ahmed's. "What kind of time is this to come home?"

Ahmed seemed to be in a daze and he mumbled incoherently.

I saw Hoyo in the doorway, holding a corner of her *sheedh* in her fist, her hand pressed to her mouth. Wasn't she going to do anything?

Abo started to really give it to Ahmed: about his attitude, his laziness, his unexplained absences. Even though I knew that most of what Abo was saying was true, my heart ached for my brother. Why didn't he speak, explain himself, defend himself? Ahmed just stood there, swaying slightly, letting Abo's words wash over him.

"Don't you have anything to say for yourself? Don't you know your mother has been worried sick about you? You think I don't know what you're up to? *Ha*? You think I'm a fool? That I was born yesterday? You ought to be ashamed of yourself!"

I thought that would be the end of it, that we would all be able to go back to bed. But then, Ahmed put his head back and looked Abo square in the eye.

"Shut up, old man," he said, slowly and clearly, "just shut the f…" He hadn't even finished saying the awful words before Abo's open hand hit the side of Ahmed's face. Ahmed swayed slightly before crashing backwards into the wall. Abo made to go after him again but Hoyo ran up behind him and held his arms, begging him to stop. I screamed then, a piercing, terrified scream; a scream that made them all look up at me, hidden in the dark on the stairs. I saw the shocked look on Hoyo's face, the tears in her eyes, the horror on Abo's face, the hurt anger on Ahmed's.

"Safia…" Hoyo called after me as I ran up the stairs, tears streaming down my face, my stomach churning, my heart tight and hurting, as if it was about to burst.

I ran into my room and slammed the door behind me. I couldn't wait to get into bed, to hide under the duvet, to shut it all out, to pretend it had never happened. But every time I closed my eyes, I saw Ahmed's curled lip as he spat out those hateful words; I heard the sickening clap as Abo's hand met Ahmed's face; I heard Hoyo's pleas, her tears as hot and painful as my own.

Hoyo tried to come in and speak to me but I had lodged my chair against the door and she couldn't get in. She gave up in the end, perhaps thinking that, if she left me to sleep, I would feel better in the morning. But I hardly slept at all and I didn't feel better when the weak sunlight hit my sari curtains.

And I felt even worse when I went down to breakfast and found only Abo, Hoyo and Abdullahi at the table, their faces tense and drawn. It didn't take me long to discover why.

Ahmed was gone.

Chapter 5

Now you depart, and though your way may lead
Through airless forests thick with hagar trees,
Places steeped in heat, stifling and dry,
Where breath comes hard, and no fresh breeze can reach –
Yet may God place a shield of coolest air
Between your body and the assailant sun.
And in a random scorching flame of wind
That parches the painful throat, and sears the flesh,
May God, in His compassion, let you find
The great-boughed tree that will protect and shade.

Sayyid Mahamed Abdillah

Ahmed had been gone for three days. Three days of sleepless nights and tears during my *salah*.

Allah, please bring him home safely, don't let anything happen to him...

Everyone else tried to carry on as normal. No one mentioned the events of that terrible night; there were no apologies, no explanations. Hoyo never said anything but I could tell that she was worried. Her routine didn't change – she still cooked and cleaned and wore her *dira'* – but there was a difference. The spring was gone from her step and she let her *dira'* trail on the floor instead of hitching one side up to show the embroidered *gogorat* underneath.

One morning, when Abo and Abdullahi had gone to pray, I walked past the boys' bedroom and heard sniffing. I pushed open the door slightly and saw Hoyo sitting on Ahmed's bed, holding one of his T-shirts to her face. It was wet with her tears. My heart ached for her, for us, for Ahmed and, in a moment, I was in her arms.

"Hoyo?" I sniffled, wiping my nose.

"Shhh, Safia, shhh," she whispered, stroking my hair. "It's OK, he'll come home soon, *insha Allah*, don't worry…"

Every hour that I was at home, I jumped to get the phone when it rang and my ears strained for the sound of keys in the lock. I kept checking Ahmed's room to see if he had come home while we were out.

When I was out, I looked for him constantly: on the bus I always went upstairs to check the seats at the back, my eyes scanning the pavements as we drove past. When I walked, I looked around all the time, hoping to catch a glimpse of his tousled head or leather jacket.

"Don't worry, Safia," Hamida had said, "he'll come home soon. They always do…"

But what if he didn't? I kept imagining my brother sleeping in a cardboard box under a bridge somewhere, hungry and scared. He acted so tough and streetwise but deep down I knew he was all talk.

I wasn't sure that he would survive out on the streets of London on his own.

Then, on the fourth day, Hamida came round to work on our English coursework.

Two weeks ago, we had the idea of designing a tabloid newspaper, featuring the exploits of all Shakespeare's characters. So far, we had written about Romeo and Juliet ('Star-crossed lovers in double suicide pact' was the headline) and were working on Hamlet. It had been my idea to put all the tragedies together as news pieces and describe the comedies in the Society pages.

"So, do we portray Hamlet as completely off his rocker or as the victim in all this?" she asked as she chewed the end of her pencil.

"Hmmm, I don't know," I mumbled before flipping over on to my bed. Hamlet was the furthest thing from my mind. I looked up at the little sheets of paper stuck all over my wall and felt an ache behind my eyes. Whenever Ahmed would come into my room, he would always look for the latest additions and read them out, either 'bigging them up' or pronouncing them rubbish.

I missed him so much. The house was like a morgue without him: his laughter, his jokes. But then, even those had been in short supply since Abo came back. I sighed and rubbed my eyes.

Hamida sat down on the bed next to me. "Are you thinking about Ahmed?"

I nodded.

"What happened when the police came over?"

"Hoyo told them that he had been missing for two days and they said not to worry, that he should be back soon."

"We see this kind of thing all the time, Mrs Dirie," the lady officer had said. "Was he having any trouble at home, any difficulties?"

Hoyo looked over at me then.

"No, not really," she said, "everything was quite normal." I had known she wouldn't tell this *cadaan* stranger what had happened between Abo and Ahmed. I looked down. If anything happened to Ahmed, I would never forgive Abo, never.

"So, you haven't heard from him at all?" asked Hamida.

I shook my head.

"Tried calling his friends?"

"Abdullahi said he spoke to a few of them but they said they hadn't seen him."

"Yeah, but they aren't going to tell *him*, are they?

They know that those two don't get along." She looked at me. "*You* should call them – they'd tell you if they knew anything."

She was right. Ahmed's friends, Faaris, Rageh, ODB and the others all knew that I was his 'little sis' and they were all as protective of me as he was. It was Faaris and Rageh who had bought me a bus ticket and called Hoyo when my bag was stolen. And if Ahmed had contacted anyone, it would have been them.

"Come on then," I said, jumping up, "what are we waiting for?"

I opened the door to the boys' room and Hamida came in after me. She wrinkled up her nose.

"So this is what teenage boys' rooms smell like, eh?"

I smiled. I had long ago grown used to the smell of sweaty socks and deodorant spray that clung to the bed sheets. "Yeah, just don't look under the bed, OK?"

I stood in the middle of the room and looked around. Where would I find Ahmed's telephone numbers? I knew looking for some sort of address book was useless: Ahmed hardly ever wrote things down anyway. I opened the drawer next to his bed and began to move the clothes around, feeling underneath them with my fingers: nothing important, just some coins and a box of matches. I opened the next one and then the third, peering under his T-shirts and tracksuit bottoms. Just then, my fingers felt something hard and smooth. I grasped it and pulled it out: his old mobile phone!

"Look Hamida!" I shouted, waving the phone at her.

"Does it still work?" she asked doubtfully.

"Yeah, it does," I replied. "I remember that he got an upgrade as soon as the new Nokia came out. He said I could have this one." I got up. "Come on, let's find a charger…"

It didn't take us long to find a charger and turn the phone on. I immediately opened his address book and began scrolling until I found Faaris' number. I took a deep breath. It wasn't my thing to call my brother's friends and, for a moment, I wondered whether I was doing the right thing, what Hoyo would say. I looked over at Hamida and bit my lip.

"It's for Ahmed," she said, her hand on my arm.

I nodded and pressed the button to call. It rang a few times, then I heard the opening lines of a rap tune I knew Faaris liked: it had gone to voicemail. I rang off and tried again.

This time, Faaris answered. "Yeah?"

"Faaris? It's Safia, Ahmed's little sister…"

"Ah, yeah, safe, *iskawaran*," he answered. "What's up, girl?"

"It's Ahmed," I said and tears stung my eyes again.

"I need to know where he is. I need to know that he's safe…" There was a long silence on the other end of the phone. "Faaris? You there?"

"Yeah, I'm here," his voice sounded guarded. "Look, Ahmed's OK, yeah? He's OK… I'll tell him to call you. Is this your number?"

I looked at the phone in my hands. "Yeah, he can call me on this number."

"OK, I'll tell him."

"Thanks, Faaris."

"No problem," was the reply.

"And Faaris?"

"Yeah?"

"Please tell Ahmed to come home…"

"I'll tell him to call you, OK, sis?"

"Ok, *asalaamu alaikum*… bye…"

★★★

Hoyo served *baasto* and *hilib* for dinner. I didn't feel much like eating but came down anyway to help Hoyo serve it.

"Here, Safia," said Hoyo, handing me a knife, "just cut up the banana for me. Make the slices thin – you know Abo likes them that way."

I took the knife and silently began to cut the bananas at an angle, arranging them on the side of the tray in a row. I liked my bananas cut thick and so did Abdullahi – but we hadn't had them that way since Abo had come back. I quickly cut a few thick slices and put them on the other side of the tray.

"OK, get the ice from the fridge, Safia, quickly – Abo and Abdullahi are waiting."

"Why doesn't Abdullahi come and help?" I asked as I took a bottle of cold water from the fridge and put it on the table along with the ice. "He always used to before."

"Ah, *'eeb*, Safia," Hoyo clucked, banging the serving spoon on the tray to dislodge a clump of *baasto*. "Abdullahi's a man now. He doesn't have any business in the kitchen... now, where's that mat for the floor?"

I had heard this many times before: as far as Hoyo was concerned, the kitchen was her kingdom and she had no interest in having men involved – not even to make themselves a cup of tea.

"A woman's pride is her kitchen," she had always said. "If she can't keep that in order, how can she keep the rest of the house in order?"

So, Hoyo ruled the kitchen – which was fine except that she often drafted me in to help her!

I preferred Ahmed's approach: if he needed something from the kitchen, he helped himself. But Abo and, lately, Abdullahi too, waited to be served.

"Safia!" I heard Abo calling me from the living room.

"*Haa*, Abo!" I answered, picking up the bottle of water and some cups that Hoyo had just finished rinsing. I took everything into the living room where Abo and Abdullahi were sitting. Abdullahi was watching the news and Abo was reading a Somali-language newspaper.

"Ah, Safia, you brought the water – good." Abo waited for me to pour him a drink of water and then took a sip.

"*Ai*, Safia, where is the ice?"

"Sorry, Abo," I murmured, mentally kicking myself for forgetting that Abo always took ice in his water, especially after a hot day. I took the cup and put a few cubes of ice into it.

"That's better," said Abo, turning back to his paper.

"Could I have a drink too, Safia?" asked Abdullahi, grinning at me. He was really trying it!

I smiled my sweetest smile and said, "Sorry, Abdullahi, I have to help Hoyo in the kitchen – but I'll leave the water here for you. If you still remember how to pour it, that is!" I spoke in English so that Abo wouldn't understand and skipped out of the door before Abdullahi could say anything else.

Just then, I heard the sound of a phone ringing

upstairs. At first, I wondered whose it was then, all of a sudden, I remembered and my heart skipped a beat. I dashed up the stairs and caught it just in time.

"Hello…?" I said breathlessly, leaning against my closed door, my heart hammering.

"*Asalaamu alaikum*, little sis," came the familiar voice.

I let out a huge sigh. To hear that voice again after so many days and so much worry was so wonderful – I wanted to hold on to the moment and keep it forever.

"Ahmed…" I breathed, "are you OK?"

"Yeah, I'm fine, sis," he replied, sniffing.

"What's wrong? Have you got a cold? Where have you been sleeping? Don't tell me you've been sleeping rough! And what about food? Have you been eating?"

My questions tripped over each other and Ahmed laughed.

"Easy, easy! One question at a time, sis! I'm fine, man, I'm fine. Just got a bit of a cold. Been stayin' at my man ODB's place cos his folks ain't around…" He paused to cough, a nasty, raking sound. "How are you, though? You been behavin' yourself?"

I laughed – Ahmed had been AWOL for four days and he was asking *me* if *I* was behaving!

"Aren't I always behaving myself?" I smiled, so glad just to be talking to him. If I closed my eyes,

I could almost imagine him sitting on the bed in my room, his smelly socks all over my duvet.

"Ahmed," I asked, "when are you coming home?"

There was a long silence and I heard Ahmed cough again.

"How's Hoyo?"

"She's OK. She's worried about you. She misses you... we all do."

"I bet Abo doesn't though," he said, bitterly.

I bit my lip. Life seemed to go on as normal for Abo. But something told me not to tell Ahmed that.

"He's worried too, Ahmed. Of course he is."

"Yeah, right, I bet he's been combing the streets looking for me, to finish what he started!"

"No, Ahmed, don't talk like that, please..." I was frightened by the hardness in Ahmed's voice. It reminded me of when he used to watch Abo eat, a look of disgust on his face.

"Sorry, little sis," he said then. "I was out of line. Don't you watch me, yeah? You keep being a good girl, listen to Hoyo and Abo..."

I became impatient then. It was all very well for him to lecture me about being a good girl and listening to our parents – but he was the one who had been coming home late, smelling strange, cursing our father. The terrible scene replayed itself in my head and I felt anger build up inside me. Why did he refuse to grow up?

"Ahmed," I said, my voice hard for the first time. "You need to sort yourself out, you know."

"Huh?" There was no mistaking the surprise in his voice. "What d'you mean, little sis?"

"Don't 'little sis' me! How come it's so easy for you to tell me how to behave but, when it comes to you, anything goes? Why can't you follow your own advice? How many times are you going to tell me not to watch you? To do as you say and not as you do? It's not right!"

He was chastened and mumbled something about taking it easy but I wasn't having it.

"No, Ahmed, all I see every day is one rule for Safia, another for everybody else: I'm sick of it. You need to come home. You need to finish college. You need to stop smoking whatever it is you smoke with Rageh and ODB. And you need to start watching yourself as carefully as you and everyone else watches me!"

I took a deep breath. I loved him too much to watch him mess his life up, but I knew I had taken a gamble. He could hang up the phone, never call again, and disappear forever. It was possible. But maybe, just maybe, I could get through to him. Maybe he would hear me, for the first time ever. I held my breath.

"You're right, little sis," he said at last, his voice

quiet and small. I breathed a sigh of relief. "Just give me a few more days, OK? Just a few more days…"

"Are you going to call Hoyo?"

"Yeah, I'll call her in the morning…"

"*Insha Allah,*" I added. "And will you call me again?"

"I'll call you tomorrow if I have enough credit. This is ODB's phone I'm using now."

"OK, I'll wait to hear from you tomorrow, yeah?"

"Yeah, OK."

"Take care, big brother," I said, half joking. But Ahmed didn't laugh. He gave *salaams* and hung up.

I was left sitting on my bed in the dark, the phone hot in my hand, my heart hammering in my chest, my own harsh words echoing in my ears.

★★★

O my brother,
Why do you swim out
To fish in deep water?
Don't you know
The current is strong there
And the sharks hungry?

★★★

Ahmed called Hoyo the day after we spoke. I heard her take the call, her voice high and faint with relief. They spoke for a short time and then Hoyo came out of the living room, dabbing at her eyes.

"So?" I said, trying to meet her gaze. "Is Ahmed coming home?"

But she refused to look me in the face as she picked something nonexistent off my shoulder.

"No, not yet." Her voice was edged with tears. "Maybe next week, *insha Allah*."

"Next week?" I cried. "Why?"

She pursed her lips. "Abo wants it that way... he thinks Ahmed needs some time away, some time to cool off..."

I stared at her in disbelief. "And what do you think, Hoyo?" I whispered, unable to believe what I was hearing.

"I think he's right, *insha Allah*..." But her voice held no conviction and I saw the sadness in her eyes. Abo had made the decision. That was all there was to it.

I was furious.

I seethed every time I looked at Abo when we sat down to eat without Ahmed. It wasn't fair! How could he come here out of the blue and start making these decisions, messing our lives up?

But Hoyo accepted it. Now that she knew Ahmed

was alive, safe, she was free to play the role of the *aroosa* once more. She began to hitch up her *dira'* again.

And I decided to stop talking to her.

One night, Hoyo came to see me before I went to sleep. She sat on the edge of my bed and held my hand, something she hadn't done since Abo had come back – she was too busy nowadays with a million-and-one things to do. But that night, she sat and tried to talk to me – about school, about Habaryero's wedding, about getting new *dira'* – everything except what *I* wanted to talk about: Ahmed and Abo. I looked at her and heard her voice in the distance and, for the first time, I felt disappointed in her. I was so far away from her at that moment, she could have been in the wilderness of Somalia for all I cared.

I thought to myself, *How can you? How can you sit here and talk to me about weddings and clothes when Ahmed has been gone for a whole week? How can you still smile with Abo when he is the one who chased him away? How can you be normal when our family is falling apart? Don't you care?*

But I was well brought-up, our Somali way. All my questions stayed inside me. I turned away. I didn't want her to see my face. And I felt ashamed for judging her; I knew that it was wrong to be angry with your own mother, the one who gave birth to you and sacrificed so much for you.

Yes, I knew all that, and still I felt anger and disappointment churn in my stomach. Just like Abo, I would never forgive her if something happened to Ahmed. Never.

***

Food sticks in my throat
Drink burns my insides
The stomach rebels
Against common sense.
Words swim before me
Ideas run for cover
The pen rebels
Against every assignment.
It's all falling down
Falling away
Falling apart.

***

"I'm concerned about your work." Miss Davies' pretty freckled face looked worried and she tucked a blond curl behind her ear for the fifth time.

We were both staring at my English homework book, open in front of us. "Quite frankly," Miss Davies continued, "this is the worst work I have ever seen you produce. Is everything all right, Safia? The Head told me that your dad came over from Somalia... is there..."

"No, Miss Davies, I'm fine," I said curtly. I was not about to discuss my family business with a teacher, not even Miss Davies. "I've just had a lot on, that's all – I'm sorry." I picked up my book. "Can I go now, Miss?"

Miss Davies looked at me then, a strange, wounded expression on her face. She looked almost disappointed that I didn't have a breakdown on the spot. Well, if she thought that I was about to spill the beans about my personal life, she was way wrong.

"Yes, Safia," she said at last. "You can go..."

I turned on my heel and walked away.

To think that only a month ago, I had been Miss Davies' star pupil! She was always bragging about me to the other English teachers and, although I begged her not to, she would often use my work as an example in class, especially in poetry lessons.

And now? I was failing my coursework and scoring the lowest marks in everything, everything but poetry. I still wrote, fiercely, hoping to let my fear and anger out somehow, in a way that wouldn't hurt anyone. Sometime, it felt like squeezing blood from a stone, painful and fruitless. But most of the time, it came out by itself: everything I wanted to say to Hoyo, Abo,

Ahmed, but knew I never would because that was not our way.

Hamida met me in the corridor. "What happened with Miss Davies?" she asked as we walked down the school steps towards the bus stop.

"Oh, nothing," I mumbled, irritated. I didn't want to talk about Miss Davies and my English homework. Besides, ever since Hamida had announced that she wanted to be a psychologist when she finished school, I wondered whether she considered me her first patient. More than once, I had felt funny about her interest in my family affairs and her desire to be as involved as possible.

"She just wanted to know why my work's been so bad lately…"

"And did you tell her?"

"Tell her what?"

"About your dad, about Ahmed…"

"No, I didn't!" I snapped. "It's none of her business what goes on in my house. It's none of anyone's business!" Hamida looked hurt then and I felt glad. I wanted her to hurt, to feel some of what I was feeling. "That's right, it's none of *your* business either, OK? Why d'you always have to be on my case, asking how I feel about this, how I'm dealing with that?"

"But Safia, I'm only trying to help…"

"But it's got nothing to do with you! It's not your problem, yeah, it's mine! And the sooner everyone leaves me to deal with it, the better!"

I had never in my life said something so mean to someone so close to me. But I couldn't take the words back. For the first time in the eight years that I had known her, Hamida's eyes filled with tears and she just stood there staring at me, her bottom lip trembling. After a moment, I couldn't bear the pain in her face so I looked down.

"I…I…I'm sorry, Hamida," I stuttered as she backed away from me, shaking her head. I tried to grab her, to let her know that I hadn't meant it, any of it, but she was too fast. She turned away and started to run, her bag full of Jacqueline Wilsons bumping against her back.

I stood there like an idiot, watching her go, tears running down my own face.

Just then, my new mobile phone rang. I jumped, thinking it was Ahmed.

"Hey, girl, what's up?" It took me a moment to recognise the voice, to realise who it was. Firdous!

"Oh, hey, Firdous," I said in a shaky voice, wiping away my tears. "What's going on?"

"Well, I saw Ahmed the other day…"

"You saw Ahmed?" I couldn't believe it. "Where?"

"Don't watch where I saw him," she answered

mysteriously. "Anyway, I managed to get your number out of him. I was wondering whether you wanted to meet up sometime? You know, have a chat?"

I thought of all the tension and misery of the past few weeks since Abo had been with us and I realised that there was nothing in the world I wanted more.

After all I'd been through, I deserved a break.

Chapter 6

I had arranged to meet Firdous at the big bus station in Stratford. Wrong move. Not only was it full of people – schoolchildren, college students, people on their way to catch their trains – but it was full of Somalis too.

Now, why was that a problem for me? Well, I didn't want to see anyone I knew. Hoyo would have assumed that I was in Whitechapel, possibly at Hamida's house. She would never have guessed that I was in Stratford on my own and, even worse, waiting to meet up with Firdous. Being here was a problem because, if anyone I knew saw me, they would most probably mention it to Hoyo. Such was the community: everyone in everyone else's business.

I saw a group of Muslim girls walking together, their arms linked. I could see from their bags that they were in high school like me but they were all wearing *abayas* and long *hijabs*. One of them was even wearing a *niqaab* that covered her face. They chatted together as they waited for their bus, their faces smiling and joking. Even the one whose face was covered was smiling – I could tell from her eyes. One of them glanced across at me and her smile broadened.

"*Asalaamu alaikum*, sis," she called over.

I lifted my hand awkwardly and did a semi-wave. "*Wa alaikum salaam*," I smiled back. They weren't Somali – they all looked Asian to me – so how come they were so friendly?

Just then, a group of schoolboys came past. I sensed a restless energy, an aggression looking for a target. You could smell it on them like sweat. Just one look at them told me that these were the kind of boys I always avoided around my estate. During the weekends, they smoked cigarettes in the lifts and had dogfights on the patchy lawn outside while their little brothers and sisters looked on.

Once, I had taken my auntie's children to the playground near our flats, just to get them out of the house while their parents were visiting. They had been having a great time on the big slide when, all of a sudden, we heard barking and a horrific growling, snarling and snapping of teeth. The children screamed and ran to me, not knowing what it was. I held their trembling bodies tight and tried to calm them. When I looked across to where the sound was coming from, I saw a whole group of kids from the estate in a circle, cheering, laughing and taking pictures with their mobiles of these two vicious dogs attacking and mauling each other. I swear I saw one draw blood.

I shivered. I would never forget that sound – ever.

The boys glanced at me but must have decided that I wasn't worth it. Besides, one of them, the tallest one, had already seen the girl in the *niqaab*.

"Oi, fellas, look!" he called out. "It's Bin Laden's missus!"

They all fell about laughing at that and I saw the girls huddle together, ever so slightly.

The boys started hissing and calling out. "Ninja! Ninja!"

"Why don't you just leave us alone?" said one of the girls, her voice shaking.

"You're the one who should leave," sneered the one in the middle. "What're you doing here anyway? Why don't you go back to where you come from – Kabul, isn't it?" He laughed harshly and the others tittered, watching to see what would happen.

"Listen mate," the one in the *niqaab* spoke then, her voice unexpectedly deep with a thick Cockney accent, "I was born here, just like you. So I ain't going nowhere, right? I've got just as much right to be here as you, OK?"

"Yeah, you Muslims got too many bloody rights! You're bloody terrorists, the lot of you!"

"You sure you ain't hiding a bomb under all that?" shouted the tall one.

"Well, there's only one way to find out, innit?" cried the other and he ran up behind one of the girls and tugged at her headscarf. Her head snapped back and her hand flew up to hold on to the front.

"Oi, don't you touch her!" shouted the one in the *niqaab*. She turned to face him, her hands on her hips but he looked her square in the eye and spat a huge gob of spit in her face. It landed on her *niqaab*, pale and glistening in the afternoon light.

I was too shocked to say or do anything but a squat, middle-aged English woman next to me had obviously seen everything.

"What d'you think you're doing?" she screeched, her face red with anger. The boys all started at her, not sure of what to make of her. "You ought to be ashamed of yourselves! Now clear off before I call the police! Go on! You make me sick!" She spat that last bit out with so much venom that the boys backed away and legged it down to the train station.

Then the woman turned to the group of girls who were all huddled around the one in *niqaab*, their faces pale, their hands shaking.

"I'm really sorry about that," she said, going up to them. "Are you all right?"

They all nodded and tried to smile but I could see that they were shaken.

I thought about the spit from that boy's nasty

mouth and I went up to the girl in the *niqaab*. "Here, d'you need something to wipe that?" I took a pack of tissues out of my bag and handed them to her.

The girl nodded, her eyes crinkled at the corners, smiling gratefully. She took a piece of tissue and turned away, dabbing at the cloth over her face.

"*JazakAllahu khairah*," she said in that deep voice. Once again, I was struck by the contrast between the strong East End accent and the Arabic words, the *niqaab* and her bravery at confronting that boy.

The others all smiled at me and murmured their thanks. Then their bus came and they were gone.

I looked behind me for a seat and an elderly West Indian woman sucked her teeth and said, "What do dem expect if dem dress like dat?"

I looked away and decided to stand.

★★★

I told Firdous about what happened as we walked to her place.

"You should have seen the one wearing the *niqaab*, Firdous!" I said. "She was fearless, man, fearless!"

"Either that or plain stupid," retorted Firdous, rolling her eyes. "I'll never get girls like that, you know. Like, why they got to be so extreme? As long as you a good Muslim on the inside, why should you have to be all covered up like them women in Saudi Arabia? Nah, man, that ain't for me!" She flicked her blonde-tipped curls and spat out her gum.

I thought about whether I agreed with her or not. Covering your face in the UK was like asking for trouble – but I didn't think that was why she was doing it.

Even though I had heard people voicing Firdous' opinion loads of times before, I couldn't forget the feeling of welcome, of genuine friendliness, when that girl had said *Asalaamu alaikum* to me, out of the blue like that.

I still had that feeling of a shared sisterhood inside me, despite Firdous' cynical words.

Auntie Iman lived on the ground floor of a quiet residential estate, nothing like the high rises down my end. In fact, it looked quiet and pretty – the neighbours grew flowers in window boxes and, a few doors down, someone was growing sunflowers. I smiled when I saw their giant heads turned to the sun.

But inside, Auntie Iman's house was a different story. It was dark and it smelled of stale cooking oil. The overstuffed chairs were a dingy green and grime clung to the walls.

This place is in need of a little TLC, I thought as Firdous threw down her bag and walked into the kitchen. I noticed she kept her shoes on so I did too.

Probably safer.

She opened the fridge and swore under her breath.

"She hasn't done the shopping, man!" She looked around at the dirty table, the sink piled high with dishes, crusty with dried cereal and pots streaked with the remains of a stew. A rickety clothes basket overflowed on to the dull grey tiles and there was a strange musty smell in the air. I walked across to the sink and tried to open a window, just to let in some fresh air, but it wouldn't budge. Greasy dust clung to my fingers and I wiped them on my skirt.

I couldn't get over the difference between Hoyo's kitchen and this one. Our kitchen was spotlessly clean, every surface shining and clutter-free. Hoyo had always said that a woman's kitchen is her pride and she had instilled that in me, so much so that I couldn't even have a cup of tea without washing and drying my cup. It was just reflex for me.

Obviously, Auntie Iman didn't feel the same way. I wondered then why she was known as 'the witch of the Ogaden'. I had only seen her a few times at family gatherings, her scarf wrapped over her chin, her eyes red and fierce. If she wasn't arguing loudly with one of my aunties, she was muttering to herself, fingering her *hijab*, jiggling her leg incessantly. Hoyo once said that Auntie Iman had seen terrible things during the war, that she was not well.

So why on earth was Firdous living with her?

"Welcome to my humble home," said Firdous, a sardonic smile on her face. "Sorry, yeah, we should have picked up some drinks from the corner shop…"

"It's OK," I replied, "I'm not thirsty anyway."

"Let's go up to my room," she said, wrinkling up her nose. She led the way up the stairs, pausing to kick some clothes down past me. "Have to wash those…" she murmured.

Firdous' room was small and cluttered and smelt of perfume mixed with dust. The walls were covered in posters – Fifty Cent, Usher, Orlando Bloom… She saw my expression when I saw that one and laughed.

"Hey, my one weakness, what can I say?"

Once again, I was struck by the contrast between Firdous' house and mine. There were no books here that I could see and no Qur'an, no prayer mat tucked away on a shelf. Just loads of cosmetics spilling over the dresser and a stack of glossy magazines. I looked around for somewhere to sit but couldn't decide between the unmade bed and the chair covered with clothes. I didn't trust the dark-coloured carpet so I perched gingerly on the side of the bed and smiled up at Firdous.

"So, how long will you be staying with Auntie Iman then?"

"Hmm, I don't know," mumbled Firdous, taking

clothes out of her bulging wardrobe. I got the feeling she didn't want to talk about it. "Here," she said at last, tossing me something on a hanger, "try this on."

I held up the strappy red dress and gulped. Me? Wear that? Hoyo would have a heart attack! *I* would probably have a heart attack, just seeing myself in the mirror!

"Go on," she cajoled, "I think it will look great on you…"

"OK then," I said, looking around for somewhere to change. Firdous saw me hesitate and laughed.

"Don't worry, I'll leave you to it. I'm going to put some clothes in the wash anyway." She got up and went to the door. "Call me when you've got it on, OK?"

When Firdous had gone, I quickly slipped the dress on over my school trousers. The top looked all right but it bunched up over my trousers. I'd have to take them off to really see how it looked.

Stepping out of my school trousers, I looked up at my reflection in the mirror and gasped. I didn't look like me. The dress was a bright red and the colour made my skin glow. It clung to curves I didn't even know I had. That wasn't Safia Dirie looking back at me, that was someone else, someone with style, someone with power – someone like Firdous.

"Wow, girl, you look good!"

I spun round to find Firdous at the door. I felt suddenly self conscious and wrapped my arms across my chest. She crossed the room and led me to the mirror. I smiled shyly as she undid my hair elastic and fluffed my hair out over my shoulders and down my back.

"You should wear your hair out more often, Safia," she crooned, "it really suits you..."

"Firdous," I said, pulling away from her, suddenly wary of what she was trying to do. "It might look nice and everything *laakinse* I wear *hijab* – and that isn't going to change." *Insha Allah*, I said inwardly.

She laughed then, a knowing laugh. "Oh, I know, I know," she said, stepping away and handing me back my hair band. "I used to wear it, remember?"

I did remember – that image in my mind of Firdous in her school uniform, her face scrubbed clean, innocent. I decided to come out with what was on my mind.

"Why did you stop wearing it?"

Firdous looked me in the eye. "Safia," she said, "it got to the stage where the *hijab* was all that I had left. I wasn't praying, wasn't doing nothing else so I thought, 'why be a hypocrite?' It's better to be straight up than hide behind your scarf..."

But I wasn't convinced. "Why didn't you just fix what needed fixing? Instead of throwing it all away?"

She looked away. "I didn't get a chance to fix anything. Uncle Ismaeel threw me out, remember? And I ended up here." She made a face.

"What's it like, living here with her?"

"Well, she's crazy, for a start. She chews *qaat* for breakfast, lunch and dinner – she says it's her medicine to make the pain go away. And you can see that domestic hygiene is not one of her interests. But I'll be leaving here soon, though, as soon as I'm old enough."

"You'll move again?"

Firdous looked at me and shrugged her shoulders. "That's been the story of my life, Safia. You know my mum and dad split up when I was only little. Hoyo lives in Holland now: she's remarried and got her own kids. Same with Abo, except he's in Canada. I haven't spoken to him in years."

Firdous' shoulders drooped and, in that moment, I saw how sad, how lonely she was.

"So how come you don't hang out with Aisha and them anymore?"

Firdous frowned and sucked her teeth. "Those *xalimos* are just haters, man, I don't have time for them. You? I like you because I think you're honest." Then she smiled. "And just cos you wear *hijab* doesn't mean you can't have fun, right?"

I nodded.

Firdous seemed to flip a switch and become someone else altogether: bouncy, giggly, girly, full of jokes and crazy stories.

And we did have fun.

We tried on loads of her clothes and she did a makeover on me, cooing all the while about my skin, my hair, my cheekbones until I told her to shut up and give me a break.

She didn't ask me about Abo, didn't ask me about Hoyo or Ahmed. I didn't have to think, didn't have to share how I felt. I was just cool, having fun.

And I liked it.

I liked it a lot.

***

You make me feel free
Free to laugh
Free to smile
Free to forget
For a while

***

Over the next few weeks, I went to Firdous' house loads of times. Hamida was off school with a cold and, besides, things were still strained between us. I went to see her once, but it was so uncomfortable, I didn't go again. I rang though, every couple of days, to fill her in on what was going on at school and all that kind of thing.

But that distance was still there. We spoke carefully, never mentioned that day at school and she deliberately didn't ask about Abo or Ahmed. A part of me was glad but another part was sad that she didn't ask me to open up.

Then I figured I would rather have fun with Firdous than pour my heart out to Hamida.

***

"I hear you've been hanging out with Firdous," said Habaryero. Ayeyo and Awowo had come to visit Abo and Hoyo to go over some details for the wedding and she had tagged along. We were sitting in my room, she as elegant as always, one leg crossed over the other, looking through a catalogue of evening dresses, bags and shoes. Habaryero was getting herself ready for married life in style.

"Yeah, just a bit," I said nonchalantly. I wasn't about to admit that I saw her at least four times a week, especially since I hadn't been asking Hoyo's permission.

"*Haa*," murmured Habaryero thoughtfully,

rubbing her forehead. Then she closed the catalogue and looked at me, a deep searching look. I made my face as blank as possible.

"Be careful, Safia," she said. "Firdous… Firdous is a lot of fun…*laakinse* she has a lot of issues, stuff, you know? I don't think you should spend time with her, I don't think your Hoyo would be pleased…"

"Firdous is all right, Habaryero, don't worry. People misunderstand her, that's all. She's really cool – we're cool…"

"I know you think you know her, Safia, but believe me, I have lived with her. There is more to her than meets the eye. Just be careful, that's all I'm saying." She reached out and stroked my face. "You're very special, Safia, always remember that. Remember who you are… and where you come from."

"I will, Habaryero," I said, "I will, *insha Allah*."

***

I thought about that conversation as I walked home with Firdous the next day. Firdous was going on about this new guy she had met, Amr.

"And he's got a friend, Safia, who'd be perfect for you, just perfect!" She squeezed my arm, more excited than I had ever seen her.

"Perfect for me?" I rolled my eyes. "What on earth

does *that* mean?"

"It means that he's a nice guy and I think he would really like you – and you would like him."

"Firdous," I said, shaking my head, "you just don't get it, do you? I wear *hijab*. Don't you think that is going to kinda scare him off?"

"No, I don't," she said shortly. "There's plenty of girls in *hijab* that have guys falling over themselves to take them out – you know you're hot anyway!"

I blushed. These last few weeks with Firdous had opened my eyes to a lot of things – and one of those things was the way in which others saw me, as a young woman.

"I'm not saying you should *marry* the guy, just meet him, that's all…" Then her eyes went all dreamy. "Do you have any idea what it's like to have a guy tell you how gorgeous you are, how much he loves you?"

Part of me thought, *yeah, right*. But the other part of me thought, *wouldn't that be wonderful?*

"I suppose it wouldn't hurt just to meet him…" I said at last.

Firdous squealed and squeezed my arm again. "That's my girl! It's going to be great, you'll see!"

***

So that's how we got to be standing on a scruffy

residential street somewhere in Forest Gate. I saw them coming from a mile away. You couldn't mistake the walk, the 'bop', the saggy pants and the lanky Somali frame.

I heard Firdous suck in her breath as she caught sight of them too. I glanced at her and saw her put on her lipstick smile, the one she always practised in the mirror at home.

They were coming closer. I looked around. Surely no one I knew would see me here of all places. I looked around again, worried this time. What if Abo saw us? Or Abdullahi? Or, even worse in its own way, Hoyo? I observed the scene from their point of view: their Safia, with the most notorious member of the family, Firdous, talking to two strange Somali boys... on the street... big-time *'eeb*!

But I didn't see anyone I knew. The street was unusually quiet, a few roads away from the hustle and bustle of Green Street. And I knew that Firdous had chosen this road on purpose. Green Street, although easier to find, was full of other Somalis, people who knew us, who knew our parents, and wouldn't hesitate to call them to give them a full report.

"*Iskawaran, walaalo.*"

I looked up and saw them in front of us: Fuad and Amr. Fuad, tall and slim, wore a black leather jacket with red and white trim. His black jeans hung dangerously low off his waist and he wore a silver ring on each little finger. I could smell his aftershave and I looked down, my face burning.

"*Nabat,* what's popping, man?"

I heard Firdous's response, her voice dripping with honey.

Fuad jerked his chin at me. "Who's your friend?" he asked.

"This is my cousin, Safia," Firdous answered, pushing me forward slightly.

"She's cute," he said. Then he turned and looked right in my face. "You're cute."

I wanted to disappear into the graffiti-scarred wall behind me. My face was flaming, my tongue thick in my mouth, so thick I couldn't speak. Shame, shame, shame! Shame on me for being so dumb! Shame on him for chatting up a girl in *hijab*! Shame on that girl in *hijab* for being there in the first place!

"Umm…er, thanks," I managed to mumble, pulling at my scarf.

"So what are you girls doing?" said Amr, his eyes sweeping Firdous's body, taking in every detail she'd been perfecting at the house. I felt embarrassed for her – didn't she feel exposed? But I could see her blossoming under his gaze. She smiled that dazzling smile of hers, the one that confused me the most, the one that said, 'I've got it all, baby', even though I knew it wasn't true.

"Ah, just hanging out, y'know, waiting for you guys to show us a good time."

"Ah, yeah?" Amr smiled. "Well, we was hoping you were going to show *us* a good time." He nudged Fuad who let out a little chuckle, his eyes never leaving my face.

This was all too much, way, way too much. Show them a good time? This had gone far enough. I started backing away, pulling Firdous by the arm.

"We really need to get home," I tried to explain. "It will be dark soon."

Firdous shot me a look and I shot her one right back. I wasn't about to stay there a minute longer and she knew it. She had to smooth things over.

"Hey, why don't we meet you guys again for a movie or something? Maybe this weekend?"

"Sure," said Fuad, still looking at me, "but only if *you* come." And he winked at me, a lopsided smile on his face.

It sounds like such a cliché but, at that very moment, I felt weak, weak in every way.

I managed to blurt out a hurried, "Maybe", before turning on my heels and walking away. I had to force myself not to run down the road. I could hear Firdous making hurried plans with them before running to catch up with me.

"Safia!" she hissed, "what is wrong with you?" I knew she didn't want them to hear us arguing so I kept walking fast, ignoring her, until we were safely on Green Street. Only then did I start walking at a normal pace… and breathing again.

"Safia," she said again, less urgently this time, reaching out to touch my arm, "what happened to you back there?"

I stopped walking. "What do you mean 'what happened'?" I snapped, my cheeks burning. "Look Firdous, I'm not like you, OK? It's one thing trying on clothes, make-up and stuff in your house – that's cool, it's fun and no one gets hurt. But meeting up with boys, going to movies, it's not my thing. Imagine if my dad had seen us! We'd be finished! Besides, Hoyo always says…"

"Hoyo?" she sneered, "you're still going by what your Hoyo says? I thought you were a big girl, Safia, big enough to make your own decisions…"

"I am, Firdous, of course I am," I said, wanting to believe it myself. "It's just that I'm not sure if this is what I want…"

"How do you know this isn't what you want?" She smiled at me then, almost kindly. "Fuad thinks you're cute – isn't that what you want? Doesn't that feel good?"

What could I say? That moment – when Fuad

had looked right at me and said those words 'You're cute' – was etched in my brain. I could hear his voice, see his stupid lopsided smile. I knew where all that was going, what it was leading to – hadn't Firdous been there a thousand times? Did I want what she had? Sure, she was free to do what other teenagers do, what all the kids at school do all the time, every weekend: dress up, go out, have fun, have boyfriends.

But Firdous also had the worst reputation, was the least respected and the most disapproved of child in my whole family. She had been kicked out by Uncle Ismaeel and was constantly in battles with Auntie Iman. Even Habaryero, never one to judge, had warned me to stay away from her. I had heard girls use the awful word '*dhilo*' about her when she wasn't there.

Was it worth the aggro from Abo, Abdullahi and everyone else?

And what about Hoyo?

At the thought of Hoyo, my heart grew cold. Hoyo? Would she even notice? Since Abo had come home, it was as if we were living on two different planets. We had never had problems between us, never, until he came along. I still wasn't really talking to her because of what had happened with Ahmed. She hadn't even noticed how little I was eating, how much time I spent away from home, how much time I spent with Firdous.

Right then, I made up my mind: I would go to the movies with Fuad. Chances are, Hoyo would never find out anyway and if she did, well, maybe then she would remember that she had a daughter, not just a husband who had come home from Somalia.

"So," I said, taking a deep breath, "when did you arrange to meet at the movies?"

★★★

Late, late that night, Ahmed came home. He came with Uncle Yusuf and my mum's cousin. He looked tired and pale, and much thinner than the last time I had seen him and he walked with a limp. Hoyo burst into tears when she saw him and held him tight.

Abo's face was stony and Uncle Yusuf asked him to step into the lounge.

I could hear their conversation from outside the door.

"Why did you bring him here?" Abo's voice was angry. "You know he has problems. And there's Safia to think about..."

Me?

"Safia is only a young girl," he continued. "I don't want Ahmed's rubbish influencing her."

"I understand that, Hassan," replied Uncle Yusuf,

"but this is not Somalia. You can't just send your child away and expect them to be OK. There are no uncles or aunties to keep him safe. There is no community to make sure he goes straight."

"He's right," added Hoyo's cousin. "If you send Ahmed away now, you will lose him. It's too dangerous out there: there's drugs, gangs, diseases... This is London, my brother, not Mogadishu."

"You have to let him come home," said Uncle Yusuf, with finality.

There was a long pause.

"All right," sighed Abo, resigned. "All right."

***

I went to see Ahmed in his room after Hoyo and Abo had gone to bed.

"Ahmed?" I whispered, tapping on the door as I pushed it open.

"Safia-girl!" he smiled weakly and turned to me. He had taken his top off and I saw the long ugly scar across his side. I gasped and tears filled my eyes.

"What happened to you, Ahmed?"

He frowned down at the scar. "Just some foolishness, sis, just some foolishness... That ODB, man," he ran his fingers through his hair. "That ODB is a real crackhead."

I nodded, my hand to my mouth, still unable to believe that the scar was real, that it had happened and I hadn't known, that this pale, thin boy was my brother for real.

"Ahmed... are you all right now?"

"Yeah, sis, I'm getting there, *insha Allah*, I'm getting there." Then he turned to me, his eyes so tired, so sad. "I just wanna catch some zzzzs now, you know?"

I nodded again. "Goodnight, Ahmed," I said as I turned to leave. "I'm really glad you're home."

"Me too, sis," came the voice from the bed. "Me too."

Ahmed slept for the next two days and, when he emerged from his room, his smile was brighter and he started praying at the mosque with Abo and Abdullahi.

Chapter 7

"Your hoyo is worried about you, you know," said Habaryero as she flipped through a magazine full of bridal hairstyles: updos, chignons, French braids and other, funkier ones like flat twists and cornrows with little shells.

We were sitting in the living room of a Somali lady who had converted one of the rooms in her flat to a hair salon. From there, she offered braiding, hair cuts, straightening, the occasional dye job and henna for brides. The house smelt of *bukhoor* and hot hair – no doubt from the straightening tongs that she heated up in a little stove for those clients who wanted to get rid of their natural curls for a while.

When she applied the red hot tongs to the hair, there was always a hiss and a small cloud of steam would rise up, carrying with it the smell of burning grease and singed hair. Sounds like torture but, for some, it was a small price to pay to be able to toss their silky straight locks at an *aroos*.

I was fortunate in that my hair was wavy and quite fine. Hoyo had forbidden me to go anywhere near the iron tongs.

"They will burn the hair off your head, Safia," she had warned me. "You have soft hair like mine – I don't want you to go ruining it."

Anyway, wearing *hijab* meant that a quick brush and an elastic band were enough for my hair. I had watched Firdous use the ceramic straighteners on her hair – and I couldn't help but laugh at all the fuss. First was the wrap lotion: smoothed on from root to tip. Then came the protective cream – to guard against the effects of the heat. Then, after the laborious and muscle-straining pulling on sections of hair all the way round with the tongs, there was the shine spray – to get it looking just right. I always found it amusing that all that effort went to waste if we happened to get caught in the rain on the way to the bus stop. Then she would pull her hood up over her head to stop it all frizzing up again and I would laugh at her.

"See?" I would say, "you might as well be wearing *hijab* like me!"

Of course, she would laugh and stick her tongue out at me.

I wondered whether she would ever wear *hijab* again.

I had heard some people say that a *hijab* is just a scarf, but to me, it went much deeper than that. It was a symbol of who I was, a way of telling the world what

I stood for. But, more importantly, it was part of my Islam, my identity. To let go of the *hijab* takes a lot. Sometimes, it's the last thing you hold on to before you lose it all completely. Wasn't that what had happened to Firdous?

But if Firdous had lost it completely, where did *I* stand? I thought about that every time I got home from Firdous' house, only to realise that I had missed my afternoon prayer, *again*. I felt sick to my heart, praying 'Asr in a frantic rush to catch the time, even as I heard the *adhan* clock announce that the next prayer, *Maghrib*, was due.

I was slipping, I could see that.

But I couldn't bring myself to do anything about it. No one around me seemed to notice anything different – to them, I was still the same Safia. But I was changing and the only other people who knew that were Hamida and Firdous. But while Hamida was critical of the changes, Firdous encouraged them. She had become the closest person to me, not because she understood me or knew my innermost thoughts like Hamida, but because she was fun to be with. She let me be whoever I wanted to be. She was my escape from all the pressure at home.

I thought about my last conversation with Hamida.

"Can you come over after school on Friday?" she had asked.

Mentally, I weighed up the pros and cons of telling her the truth about my plans, that Firdous and I were going to the movies with Fuad and Amr. But we had made up since our fight and I decided to come clean.

"Firdous and I are meant to meet these guys for a movie…" I said quietly, watching her expression carefully.

"Whaaaat?" she breathed, a horrified look on her face. "Does your mum know about this?"

I shook my head. "Of course not, Hamida, be serious!"

She looked at me then, her eyebrow raised. "Why are you doing this, Safia?" she said at last. "What are you trying to prove?"

I shrugged. "It's just a movie, Hamida…"

She laughed then. "You and I both know that it's never 'just a movie'." Then she was serious again. "Are you going to take off your *hijab*?"

"Of course not!" I retorted. "Hamida, don't worry, I'm not about to go wild. I just want to know what it's like to be like everyone else."

"I'm not like everyone else," said Hamida quietly. "You never wanted that before." Then she smiled ruefully. "But I suppose you have to discover that for yourself. I'm not supporting you in this, you know, but I know that you're going to do it anyway. Just be careful, yeah?"

The night before, I had tried to get Ahmed on my side. He had sent me a text, asking me to bring him some fried chicken and chips on my way home. He had lost so much weight, I was happy to bring him whatever he wanted to eat and I smiled as he tore open the box hungrily.

"You want some?" he asked, shaking the box my way.

"No, thanks," I said. I watched him eat for a while, then said, "Ahmed, what do you think of Somali girls who go to the movies, you know, with guys..?"

Ahmed's eyebrows shot up immediately. "Nah, sis, don't you even be thinking along them lines. It's just asking for trouble. You know that it ain't allowed and, besides, if I ever catch a guy trying to mess with you, I'll kill him, OK? No man's gonna be chirpsing my sister cos all of them got sick, dirty minds. Believe me, I know!"

I couldn't confide in Ahmed, either.

I shook my head and looked at the page in front of me. I wanted Habaryero to have her hair braided in little plaits, possibly with beads on the ends. She always looked so pretty with that style – she reminded me of a picture I saw once of a Somali nomad, shy and pretty in a really natural way. But Habaryero wasn't keen on the idea.

"It's my wedding day, Safia," she had reminded

me, "I want something special, something different…"

"Like this you mean?" I had said, pointing to a woman with short Afro hair dyed blonde.

"Not that different!" she laughed, slapping my leg. "Imagine what the aunties would say about that! But did you hear what I said about your mum?"

"What did she say, Habaryero?"

"She says you've been very distant lately, not talking much, not yourself, you know?"

"I'm not sure what she's talking about, Habaryero," I replied quietly. But Habaryero noticed my defensive look and made me turn to face her. She looked deep into my eyes. I looked away. Habaryero was just too intuitive by far.

I could feel her eyes on me as I started flipping through the magazine again but she didn't say anything for a long time. I was aware of her getting up to go the kitchen and I looked up then, relieved. When she came back, she had two cups of tea and she handed me one.

"Thanks, Habaryero," I said, even though the hot cup burnt my fingers and the sweet tea scalded my lips.

"Safia," she said finally, "I think you should get out more."

I looked up at her in surprise. "Get out more?" I asked. "What do you mean?"

"You need to meet more girls your own age, do more stuff, be exposed to different things. I have a friend who I used to go to college with – Umm Abdullah – and she's set up a youth group for Somali girls. They meet every Friday afternoon. She asked me to invite you to go along…"

"I don't know about that, Habaryero," I said warily. "I really don't think that's my kind of thing."

"But how do you know, Safia?" Habaryero's voice was soothing, persuasive. "How will you know unless you try it?"

"I just don't find the idea of spending my Friday afternoon at a youth group very appealing, that's all."

"Why, have you got other plans, young lady?" She nudged me and I grinned sheepishly. Immediately, I felt a stab of guilt. I couldn't even be honest with Habaryero about where I was going.

Then I had an idea – a brilliant idea. I was sure Hoyo and Abo would give me permission to go to Habaryero's youth group. I could simply leave early and catch the movie with Firdous and the guys. No one would ever know that I hadn't stayed for the whole thing and it meant that I could keep everyone happy.

I smiled up at Habaryero who was still watching me. "OK then," I said brightly, "I'll give it a try, *insha Allah*."

She smiled broadly. "OK, I'll tell Umm Abdullah to expect you. Here, let me write down the address for you." I looked over her shoulder as she wrote and I mentally calculated the distance from the address to the movie theatre.

★★★

Weaving
Weaving
A web of lies and stories.
Be careful
Be careful
It could get sticky.

★★★

"What d'you mean you might be a bit late today? Are you bailing out on me?"

"No, Firdous," I said, trying to calm her down. "I just have to take care of something first, that's all. I'll be there before the movie starts; I just won't be able to go eat with you guys, that's all."

"Are you sure, Safia, cos Amr said that Fuad's looking forward to seeing you – you don't want to let him down, right?"

I blushed and ducked my head. "Nah, I'll be there.

I'll chat to you later, yeah, I've got to go."

I looked at Habaryero's neat handwriting on the scrap of paper in my hand. The place wasn't far – I would make it on time if I walked quickly.

***

The room where the youth group was meeting was in a small, rundown office block that backed on to a warehouse. Trains rumbled over the bridge above it. I saw a few Somali girls pushing a big green door on the ground floor so I figured we were all going to the same place. We smiled shyly at each other and exchanged greetings when we got to the top.

The room itself was a pleasant change from the shabby courtyard outside. Here, big windows lined the walls and the polished wooden floor was clean. There were some chairs arranged in a circle so I took one nearest the door. My heart thumped as I thought of my plan.

I looked at the other girls in the room, wondering whether anyone could see my ulterior motive, but they all seemed busy with other things. There was quite a mix: younger girls still in uniform, some with glasses, some with braces; girls my age, some in long dark scarves, some in bandanas. I caught sight of one girl who looked different to the others. For a start, I was sure she wasn't Somali. She was very light-skinned and her eyes were slanted, as if she had Chinese somewhere in her family. She sat with another Somali girl, both of them in very neat *hijabs*, pinned on the shoulder, with black *abaayas* and sports shoes. The two of them were talking and I could hear the fair-skinned one saying, "*Na'am, walaalo, na'am.*" That made me even more curious: an *ajanib*, speaking Arabic and Somali? What was *that* all about?

Just then, I heard a loud, "*Asalaamu alaikum, girls!*" from behind me and I looked around to see a Somali lady in a traditional half *jilbab* striding into the hall, a chubby little boy slung up on one hip and a gorgeous smile on her face. Everyone turned to her and returned her greeting warmly. I smiled instinctively, and that warm feeling of sisterhood came back for a moment.

She walked to the middle of the circle and smiled again, shifting the baby so that he sat higher on her side.

"I'm sorry I'm late everyone, *astaghfirullah*," she said breathlessly. "Are you all OK?"

We all nodded.

"Right, OK, let's get started then. First, I see we have some new faces here today…"

She looked at me enquiringly. I felt myself blush as all the girls turned to me. "What's your name, *ukhti*?"

she asked.

"Safia," I answered, way too softly. "Safia Dirie. My aunt, Na'ima, told me about the group."

The lady's face lit up again. "Ah, of course," she cried, "*Masha Allah*! Welcome to our group – so glad you could make it."

The others smiled at me encouragingly.

"And you, *ukhti*?" She turned to the girl with the Chinese eyes. "What's your name?"

"Hi… *as-salam-alikum*," she said, faltering on the Arabic words, "I'm Lisa… I'm a new Muslim…"

"A new Muslim? *Masha Allah*!"

"You mean your parents aren't Muslim?"

"Wow…for real?"

"Welcome to the *deen*, *ukhti*!"

Lisa's words had caused quite a stir. I had never met a convert before. Sure, I had heard of famous converts like Malcolm X and Muhammad Ali and even hip hop stars like Mos Def and the boxer Danny Williams. But I had never met one in the flesh – and definitely not a girl my age.

"How old are you, little sister?"

"Fifteen…" was her reply.

"And what religion were you before?"

"Nothing really – just a party girl, I guess." Lisa grinned. "*Alhamdulillah*, Allah guided me – no more guys and miniskirts, eh?" She nudged the girl next to her and they both giggled.

Everyone was full of questions for Lisa, and Umm Abdullah had to try several times before she got our attention.

"OK, OK, girls, take it easy! You can ask Lisa your questions later, let's get on with the session, OK?"

We all settled down, although I couldn't help looking over at Lisa admiringly. Here was a girl who had been a typical teenager – a 'party girl' – and, without any pressure from parents, community and all that, she had become a Muslim! Now, I love my religion but even I have to admit that it isn't the easiest way of life. But she had made that change – and from what I could tell, she looked pretty serious about it too. I knew girls who were born and raised Muslim who didn't cover their hair, let alone cover their clothes with an *abaayah*! Briefly, I imagined what Firdous would make of Lisa. Firdous was going after everything Lisa had left behind – there couldn't have been a starker contrast.

Umm Abdullah began handing out some forms. "Please keep one and pass the rest along. This is the letter for your parents about the trip to Manor House."

"Is that the one you told us about last week?" The girl sitting next to Lisa spoke.

"Yes, that's right, Maryam," Umm Abdullah

answered. "It's all confirmed, *masha Allah*, and we've booked the coach. Now all you need to do is get your parents to sign the consent forms. Do you think that's going to be a problem?"

"Nah, I done told Hoyo about it – she's cool about it," said a girl in a tracksuit, putting the form in her bag.

"Yeah man, blatant!" said a girl sitting next to her who was wearing a smart black *hijab* and a denim jacket. "D'you remember last summer?"

"The midnight walks? And the campfire?"

"That was rough! What about the midnight feasts?"

"I liked the food best…"

"I loved beating you at tennis…"

"It was really nice to all pray together, *masha Allah*…"

"I'm definitely going, man, no doubt!"

"What about you, Zahra?" Umm Abdullah asked a pretty girl wearing a blue half *jilbab*. "Will your parents let you come?"

"*Insha Allah*, it shouldn't be a problem. My mum knows you and she trusts me so she's fine about it…"

But not everyone was happy.

"Auntie, it's not fair," said a young girl in braces. "My mum said it's '*eeb* for a girl to sleep outside her dad's house. Is that true, Auntie?"

"Yeah, my dad said the same thing, you know! Can't you talk to them for us, please?"

"Yeah, we really, really want to come!"

"OK, girls," said Umm Abdullah at last, "I'll try – but I can't promise anything!"

I wondered whether Hoyo would let me go on the trip. It sounded like fun – and the girls seemed nice too. And I really wanted to find out more about Lisa. I folded my form carefully. I would get Habaryero to convince Hoyo, *insha Allah*.

The rest of the session passed quickly. Umm Abdullah gave a presentation on personal hygiene for Muslim girls (washing after your period, shaving and stuff like that) and we all talked about our favourite subjects at school. It was relaxed and friendly and I found myself enjoying it a lot.

When it was time to pray *'Asr*, some of us went to make *wudhu* in the tiny bathroom.

"Has anyone got a bottle for *istinja*?" asked one girl.

"Here, use this one," replied another, handing her a small drinking bottle full of tap water.

"What's *is-tin-ja*?" I turned to find Lisa next to me, a confused look on her face.

"Oh, it's when you wash yourself after you use the toilet," I told her.

"Ah, seen," she said, nodding. "Safe..."

"So, have you found it difficult, learning all the rules and stuff?" I really wanted her to tell me why she had left a 'normal' life to be a Muslim.

"It's amazing," she said, smiling. "Every day I learn something new, something that makes me even happier and prouder to be a Muslim."

"*Masha Allah*, that's really lovely," said Zahra, the girl in the blue half jilbab who was now standing next to me. "You put us born Muslims to shame, you know. May Allah make us all stronger, *ameen*."

Ameen, I said inwardly, *ameen*.

We all prayed together in rows, our feet and shoulders pressed together, our movements synchronized as we raised our hands, bowed, prostrated.

In the last *raka'a*, the silent room was suddenly filled with the sounds of Usher's latest single. I cringed. I had told Firdous not to download that stupid ringtone! But it kept ringing, obscenely loud, and I began to pray that the sister would finish the prayer quickly so that I could go and switch it off.

As soon as the prayer was over, I ran to my seat and pressed the 'silent' key. Only then did I answer it.

"Safia, where are you?" Firdous' voice was shrill. "We've been waiting for ages, hurry up!" She hung up.

I looked at my watch and gasped. Was that the time? I looked around quickly. Everyone seemed to be busy, making *dhikr* or folding up their prayer gowns and the big mat on the floor. Others were in the kitchen, preparing the food. I hesitated. I wanted to stay here, in this warm, friendly place, with these nice sisters. I bit my lip. Maybe I could cancel with Firdous after all.

Then the phone vibrated and I answered it before it could ring.

"Hello?" I answered it, keeping my voice low.

"Hey, girl, what's poppin'? What's up with keeping a guy waiting like this?"

It was Fuad.

My pulse started racing as I looked around one more time.

"I'm coming," I said and grabbed my bag, walking quickly to the exit, looking back once I was out of the door to make sure no one had seen me.

Then I rushed down the stairs of the block and started running down the road.

By the time I got to the movie theatre, I was hot and sweaty. Just outside the building, I tried to get my breath back. I dabbed at my face with a tissue from my bag. When I looked up, I saw Firdous coming towards me, followed by Fuad and Amr.

Firdous had obviously made a huge effort and I could tell that Amr appreciated it by the way he looked at her.

I felt embarrassed by my *hijab*. Although I had tried to funk up my normal look with some bangles and a low slung belt, I knew that I looked like a kid next to Firdous. I heaved a big sigh. But then I saw Fuad smiling at me with that lopsided smile and my heart skipped a beat. What was it that Firdous had said about girls in *hijab* who had guys dying to take them out? Well, maybe I was one of those.

"Hey girl," Firdous hugged me and I smelt her perfume, as cloying as always. *Honestly, Firdous, did you have to make it all so obvious?* But I smiled and hugged her back.

"Come, let's go," said Amr, "the movie's about to start."

We all turned to go up the steps to the theatre, Amr with his arm around Firdous, Fuad walking close beside me. I took a deep breath and pushed open the theatre door.

***

The movie theatre was full of kids, eager to get a headstart on the weekend. A rowdy group of girls, still in their uniforms, their ties loose around their necks, talked loudly on their mobile phones and threw popcorn at each other.

There were other couples there, a few big groups

and some Somalis too. But I didn't see anyone else in *hijab*.

This is wrong, Safia, you shouldn't be here.

But Fuad had taken my hand and was pulling me to where we were going to sit. My face felt flushed and my hands clammy and, as soon as we sat down, I wiped them on my skirt.

No one spoke as the opening credits appeared on the screen.

The movie began and I looked at the screen, intently, trying not to think of Firdous and Amr who were not watching the movie any more.

This is wrong, Safia, you shouldn't be here.

The main character made a funny speech and I laughed, trying not to think of Fuad's arm around the back of my seat, his hand on my shoulder.

This is wrong, Safia, you shouldn't be here.

I felt Fuad's fingers stroking my shoulder and I shivered, trying not to think of my knees that had turned to jelly.

But then, as if from nowhere, the sound of Hoyo's voice was in my ears. "You are special, Safia, you always will be. Don't give yourself away like something cheap." And suddenly, it came to me, with blinding clarity, what I was doing, what I was about to let happen. I pulled away from Fuad's hand, shaking.

"No, Fuad, no..." I stuttered, shaking my head.

When I saw the amused look on his face, I realized how babyish I sounded and my face burned. I tried to play it cool while I fumbled around in the dark for my bag. I couldn't wait to get out of there.

"Sorry, but I'm not feeling this," I whispered, trying to make my voice sound normal. "This movie's wack anyway. I'm going to go now…"

Fuad frowned slightly then shrugged his shoulders. "Sure, girl," he said, coolly, "whatever you say…" And he got up and followed me out to the aisle. I could feel his eyes on me. It was strange: whereas before that look had made me weak in the knees, now it made me feel exposed and vulnerable. I didn't want to imagine what thoughts were running through his head.

"I done told you, sis, guys have got sick, dirty minds! Don't you fall for none of their foolishness!" Ahmed's voice echoed in my head.

I glanced over at Firdous, still in Amr's arms, and I shook my head. I would call her later.

When Fuad and I stepped out of the building, the late afternoon sun was blindingly bright. I had to stop and blink for several minutes before everything looked normal again.

"Do you want me to drive you home?" asked Fuad, jingling the keys in his jacket pocket.

"Nah," I said, as casually as I could, "I think I'll just take the bus." Really, I just wanted to get as far away from him as possible.

"OK, then, I'll walk you to the bus stop."

"You really don't have to do that," I said quickly. I started walking, fast, looking straight ahead, trying to make him get the message.

Then, out of the corner of my eye, I saw a Ford Fiesta, a Nile green one. My heart almost stopped beating. I had only ever seen one Nile green Ford Fiesta in my life and the person who owned it was one of the last people I wanted to see me there in that car park with a strange Somali boy with an earring in his ear.

And, sure enough, seconds later, Uncle Yusuf stepped out of the car. He shaded his eyes from the setting sun and looked around the car park until he was looking directly at me.

"Down!" I hissed at Fuad as I dived behind the nearest car, pulling him down beside me. I pressed my body against the car, my heart hammering, sweat prickling my back, my throat dry with fear.

Uncle Yusuf could *not* see me here. For several minutes, I stayed like that, crouched against the car, listening for Uncle Yusuf's footsteps crunching in the gravel.

"Who's that?" Fuad asked, jerking his head to the side.

"My uncle," I whispered.

"Is he tight?" asked Fuad.

I nodded, hardly daring to speak. "If he finds me, I'm finished."

"Come on, follow me," whispered Fuad, taking my hand again. I was so scared that I let him lead me once more, staying low between the cars so as not to be seen.

"Where are we going?" I asked.

"My car's just over there," answered Fuad, pointing towards a quiet corner of the car park.

Ducking and diving between the parked cars, we finally made it to Fuad's Golf. He quickly unlocked the doors and we scrambled in, shutting the doors as quietly as we could behind us.

Once inside, I was able to try breathing normally. Under ordinary circumstances, this would have been quite funny but now, my only question was whether Uncle Yusuf had seen us or not. If he hadn't, *alhamdulillah*, I had managed to avoid any consequences for my moment of madness.

But then, as I began to calm down, I became more aware of the fact that I was now alone in a car, in a remote part of a car park with a guy that I hardly knew, a guy who kept looking me up and down, a slow burn in his eyes.

"So," he said softly, flipping a switch on the car radio, "how do you feel now? A bit more relaxed?"

"Hmm," I said, chewing my lip, "I suppose so…"

"Good," he said, and he shifted in his seat to sit closer to me.

And then I realised what he had in mind and a chill ran through my veins.

Oh, Allah, please don't let this be happening to me. Not to me.

Hadn't I made it clear that I wasn't up for that? That I wasn't like that? I pushed him away but he held my wrists, so hard I felt like they would snap between his fingers.

"Don't pretend, girl," he crooned. "You know this is what you wanted."

"No, please," I begged, "it was a mistake! Just a mistake! I'm sorry!"

"Well, I don't like girls who try to play me," he snarled. "You're just like your cousin – only difference is that you pretend and she doesn't."

"No, seriously," I cried, panic rising inside me. "You've got me all wrong!"

"Yeah, whatever…"

Before I knew it, he was on top of me. I struggled against him, panic growing inside me.

What was he trying to do?

But I didn't have time to think about it. I had to save myself, had to get out of there. I took a deep breath and screamed, screamed for someone, anyone to hear me and get me out of the nightmare.

And my heart cried out: *Please, Allah, help me, save me!*

Fuad clamped his hand over my mouth but I bit down, hard. He swore at me and raised his hand. It all happened in slow motion: I saw the sweep of his hand as it rose in the air, then it swung down towards me, crashing into the side of my face. My head snapped to the side against the window and I felt heat, then pain spread through my cheek. Then, all of a sudden, the door was open and the air hit my face with a rush. I opened my eyes and tried to focus and, there by the car door, his hands rolled into fists, murder in his eyes, was Abo.

Chapter 8

Abo let out a huge roar and lunged at Fuad.

"*Kalab!*" he shouted as he dragged him out of the car. "You dog, what are you doing to my daughter?"

Fuad stammered, trying to defend himself as Abo held him by the neck but he was silenced by a blow to the shoulder. Fuad's face contorted with pain as he hunched over and slid down against the car. Abo was shouting at him in Somali, cursing him.

"If you ever come near my daughter again, I will kill you, do you understand? You will be dead! Dead!"

I was curled up on the car seat, shaking, shocked. I heard the sickening thuds as Abo kicked Fuad. I was terrified of what Abo would do once he had finished with Fuad. I mean, how it must have looked: his daughter in a car with a boy in a car with steamy windows. Would he beat me? Throw me out? Kill me?

But I was innocent! This wasn't what I wanted, wasn't what I planned. I had just made a terrible, awful mistake. And I started to cry.

Abo finished with Fuad and turned to me. He saw that I was fully-clothed and winced when he saw my swollen cheek. He spat on the ground near Fuad's head then turned to go.

"*Kaale!*" he said sternly and I followed him to where Uncle Yusuf's car was parked.

He was sitting in the driver's seat and didn't look at me once.

I got into the back seat and sat there, crying silently, until we reached our block of flats.

Abo thanked Uncle Yusuf and then he left, looking at me one last time. I couldn't read his expression. Pity? Disgust? I wasn't sure.

Abo opened the door to the building and I held my breath as the stench of the chute hit me full in the face. The smell was always worse after a hot afternoon.

I looked at my reflection in the mirrored walls of the lift. In between all the graffiti and crude messages, I saw a scared-looking brown-skinned girl with a swollen cheek, red, puffy eyes and a trembly chin. She stood next to a tall, stern-faced man with grey speckles in his beard. She looked better than how I felt.

I was still shaken by all that happened and all I wanted was to get up to my room, make *wudhu* and pray.

"Allah is *Ar-Rahman*, the Most Merciful," Hoyo had told me once, "and He loves to forgive. He created us and He knows that we are weak so no

131

matter what you have done, be sure that Allah will forgive you..."

I knew that the prayer wiped away sins, washed them away like water, and I desperately needed to wash now, to cleanse myself of everything that had happened. Yes, the prayer was what I needed most right then.

But some would wonder why. All I had done was go to the movies with a guy and, as for what had almost happened after, that wasn't my fault. But I knew that it wasn't that simple. I knew that a Muslim girl was meant to keep herself in line and that a Muslim boy was meant to do that too. I knew that dating wasn't part of Islam or the *daqaan*, that it was single or married, no in-between. And I had never had a problem with that. And then all that changed. Because of a lopsided grin and a tired line like 'You're cute', I had compromised my principles. I thought of Firdous and Amr and felt sick. What was she doing? What was she looking for?

I needed to pray and I decided then and there that, when I prayed, I would pray for Firdous too. I had never thought of her as lost before but the thought occurred to me then.

To pray, to cleanse, that was what I needed.

Abo didn't say a single word to me until we got into the house. He murmured a greeting to Hoyo and told her briefly what had happened: that Uncle Yusuf had seen a boy following me and called him. He told her what had been happening when he found us. Hoyo's eyes were wide with shock and concern as she looked past Abo at me standing in the corridor.

"Go and see your Hoyo," said Abo shortly as he slipped off his shoes and went upstairs to their room.

Hoyo pulled me into the kitchen. "What happened, Safia?" she said, looking at my bruised face. "What happened?"

I started to cry then, huge sobs that made it impossible to talk.

Hoyo kept asking questions: "Where were you?" "What happened to your face?" "Where have you been?" "Why weren't you at the youth club?"

I couldn't answer. I just kept crying. I wanted to speak, to tell her that I was sorry, that it wasn't what it looked like, that nothing happened, but I couldn't find the words. And I thought about Firdous: the escape she had offered, how she had seemed to have everything, how I had yearned for just a taste of what she had – and how bitter it had turned out to be.

You've let yourself down. You've let everyone down.

I thought about Hoyo, Abo, Abdullahi, Ahmed, my reputation, all my fine principles and all I could say was, "I'm sorry, Hoyo, I'm sorry."

Then I felt the pain of the past month rush

through my body like a tidal wave, and all my deepest feelings of sadness, anger, jealousy, guilt, shame and remorse roared in my ears. I needed to let it out, I needed desperately to speak, to let out all that was clogging up my insides. But I didn't know how. I heard the voices of aunties and elders: honour your hoyo – obey your hoyo – don't disgrace your hoyo – paradise lies at the feet of your hoyo – and I was afraid of Hoyo's reaction so I just kept sobbing.

Hoyo stepped back, alarmed at my violent tears. She had never ever seen me this upset.

"Safia?" she said, fearfully, reaching out to touch my shoulder. "What is it? What's wrong?"

"There was a boy, Hoyo. He tried…"

"Tried what, Safia?" Her voice was sharp.

"It was a mistake, Hoyo," I said through my tears. "It wasn't my fault… he tried to force me…"

"Force you?" Hoyo was shocked. "Are you OK? Did he make you do anything?"

"No, Hoyo, Abo found me just in time…"

"*Alhamdulillah*," she breathed. Then, she put her arms around me and held me close. She hadn't done that in such a long time, it made me cry even more. I clung to her and she rocked me gently, murmuring, her lips against my head.

Slowly, the tears slowed down and I was able to look up at Hoyo.

"Safia," she said again, "what's been happening to you? Where did my little girl go? You've changed – I feel like I don't know you any more…"

Hoyo's voice was sad as she stroked my cheek. Maybe, just maybe, I would be able to tell her how I felt, to confide in her …maybe? It was worth a try.

"Hoyo," I began, slowly, sniffing, choosing my words carefully. "I know how happy you have been since Abo came back. I can see it. And I'm glad for you. It's just that, for me, it hasn't been that great… In fact, it's been really awful…"

She frowned then and I hesitated, wondering whether or not to continue. But then I saw that her frown was not one of anger but of incomprehension, and I continued.

"Of course I was happy too when you told us Abo would be coming home – we all were. But when he did come, everything changed: you changed, Abdullahi changed, Ahmed changed and… and I changed. All of a sudden, I wasn't part of things any more. I was shut out all the time. I don't know anything about Somalia or politics – does that mean I don't have anything to say? I felt that Abo didn't have time for me, that he wasn't interested in me at all."

"Of course he was, Safia," Hoyo began – but I continued.

"But I could have handled that, Hoyo, it was OK,

really. It was what happened with Ahmed that made it worse. I blamed Abo for making him run away and… and when you told me that Abo didn't want Ahmed to come home, I couldn't take it: I was angry with him and I was angry with you…" I said the last bit quietly, looking at the floor, waiting for her reaction, knowing that this was *'eeb*, not done, not acceptable to be angry with your parents.

Hoyo sighed but was silent, waiting for me to continue.

"You were so busy with being a wife again and preparing for Habaryero's wedding that you didn't notice me: you didn't notice that I was hardly ever around, that I wasn't eating, that I was doing badly at school. I felt like you didn't need me any more, that I wasn't special to you, now that Abo was back. It's like he became your whole world…" My voice trailed off as I remembered the loneliness of sitting in my room on my own while Hoyo and Abo spoke softly downstairs, drinking cups of sweet tea on the kitchen floor. I looked up at Hoyo and she was quiet, thinking, holding my hand and stroking it for a long time. I didn't say anything: I waited, sniffing, listening to the ticking of the clock and the faraway traffic from the street outside.

Then, finally, Hoyo spoke. "Safia, I never told you the story of how your father and I got married, did I?"

I sniffled and shook my head.

"Ayeyo and Awowo had always planned that I would marry someone from our town, from the same *qaabil*, as they had done. In fact, men from our *qaabil* had been asking about me since I was fourteen years old and could cook *suqaar*. But I was stubborn. I refused them all – I knew they weren't right for me. So I waited while my parents became more and more frustrated, worried I would be left behind while other girls my age were on their second, third, fourth babies.

"Then one day, Awowo became very angry with me. I think it was because he had just received the news that his brother's youngest daughter was getting married. Ayeyo too was ashamed that she should still have an unmarried daughter. It was *'eeb*, it wasn't right, and the neighbourhood gossips tore my mother's flesh with their rumours.

"Well, anyway, Awowo sent my mother to tell me that he swore *wallahi* that he would marry me to the next man to walk through the door, whether I liked it or not. I thought then, maybe I had made a mistake, maybe I should have married Ismaeel, the carpenter's son.

"But the next man to come to speak to my father was tall and handsome, with a soft voice and wavy hair. *Wallahi*, I caught sight of him in the compound and my heart missed a beat."

I shifted then, a bit embarrassed, aware that Hoyo had never, ever spoken to me like this before. But I wanted her to continue, wanted to hear who the handsome stranger was.

"Well, my youngest cousin raced to me in the kitchen to tell me that Hassan Maxamed was speaking to Abo, speaking to him about me."

I let out a little gasp. Abo?

Hoyo smiled at me. "Yes, Safia, that was your father. But Awowo was not pleased at all. I could tell from the deep frown on his face when I brought him his *qahwa*. Ayeyo looked worried and kept wringing the cloth of her *dira'*, glancing up again and again at my father's angry face."

"Why, Hoyo, why?" I couldn't think why my grandparents weren't pleased for Hoyo – they had wanted her to get married, hadn't they?

"Your father's family were from the same *qaabil* but they were desert people, nomads. My parents didn't think his family were honourable or rich enough for their daughter, even though Abo offered a very good dowry for me. As you know, in the Somali *daqaan*, a marriage is between families, not just individuals so, for them, the status of the family was even more important than the fact that your father was educated and was building his own house."

"But why didn't they just refuse to allow it?" I was

baffled. After all, without the parents' consent, no Muslim marriage could go ahead: everyone knew that.

Again Hoyo smiled. "*Haa,*" she said, "but remember that your grandfather took an oath: he swore *wallahi*. And the imam told him that that was it. He had taken an oath and he had to stick by it. So they had to consent to the marriage even though the family was outraged. Some family members threatened to disown me, to cast me out, some cursed me and told me my children would be no better than mongrel dogs.

But you know what, Safia, I didn't care. I saw something in your father; I saw it in his eyes, in the way he walked, the way he carried himself, that he was different. And I prayed, Allah! I prayed so hard for Allah to show me the right thing to do. And so I married him and left my parents' home. And the minute I stepped into your father's house, my arms heavy with gold, my fingertips stained black with henna from Yemen, my eyes made smoky with *kohl* from Mecca and I glanced into your father's face, I felt safe. It was as if I had come home..."

Her voice trailed off, far-off memories misting her eyes. She continued to speak, on and on, describing the little house my father had built for her, how he taught her how to read, how tenderly he looked after her when she was heavy with their first child,

Abdullahi.

"And when I had you, Allah, you should have seen his face! You would think his daughter was Bilqees, the Queen of Sheba. He loved you so much, he was so proud to have a daughter who looked like the two of us. We were happy then, *wallahi*, so happy that Hoyo and Abo changed their minds about the marriage. They soon grew to love your father like their own son…"

I followed her story, breathless, sometimes forgetting that this was my mum and dad she was talking about. It sounded like a romance from a storybook, full of intrigue, family feuds … and the kind of love that could change the world.

"What about the rest of the family?" I asked.

"Well, there are always those who hate to see others happy – so the gossips kept talking. And then the war came, and everything changed."

I shivered when I heard Hoyo's voice change.

"People were dying every day, Safia. Somalis shooting other Somalis, people being robbed at checkpoints, women being taken as slaves and worse, children disappearing: it was a terrible time. We were afraid, so afraid. Your father wanted to send us away with my mother and father but I refused. 'We live together or we die together,' I told him. I was not going to abandon him in Mogadishu, where the warlords could shoot you if they didn't like your face.

"But the situation became bad, Safia. Abo insisted that we had to leave, so we packed up a few things and made our plans to join Ayeyo and Awowo who were in Kenya by that time.

"But, *subhanAllah*, it was not meant to be. The car we were riding in was ambushed and we all found ourselves out on the dusty road with guns pressed against our heads."

Hoyo was shaking now, her voice trembled, reliving every detail. "Abdullahi and Ahmed were crying, clinging to Abo as the soldiers questioned him. They had tied his hands behind his back and he struggled to keep his balance as they pushed him from side to side. 'What is your tribe? Where are you going? This one,' said one of the soldiers, 'this one is one of those dirty *midgaan* – you can see it in his face!'

"You were too young to know what was happening and you were hungry. You kept pulling at my *dira'* because you wanted milk. When I didn't give it to you, you started screaming and one of those soldiers told me to shut you up before he did. 'She's a baby!' I shouted at him. 'She needs to eat!' Then I cursed his parents and forefathers and turned my back to him and sat down to feed you.

"My heart, Safia, my heart was beating like a thousand racing camels. Maybe he would shoot me right there? But no, they were still questioning Abo: his clan, his politics, how much money he had... With every answer he gave, I could see them going more and more crazy. I had heard about these militiamen – I knew that they were high on *qaat* most of the time and I was afraid, so afraid that they would kill us all. Then one of their commanders drove up and yelled at them. 'What the hell are you doing? Stop wasting time with these cockroaches! Bring that man in and kill the rest of them!'

"They started pulling Abo towards the van and I jumped up, my heart in my mouth. 'No!' I screamed as I ran towards them, 'don't take him! Please don't kill him!' I grabbed Abo's arm and held on, hitting out at the soldiers. I was like a wild animal. They tried to push me away but I hit out, kicking and spitting until one of them hit me in the head with his rifle butt. Everything went black.

"When I awoke, they had gone. It was nearly dark and you children were huddled around me, asleep. It was by the grace of Allah that a truck passed by, full of other people fleeing, on their way to Kenya. I bribed the driver with one of the rings your father had given me and they took us to Kenya, to the refugee camps there. After many months, we found Ayeyo and Awowo and, from there, we were able to come to Britain. That is when your memories start, *alhamdulillah.*"

I drew a ragged breath. So much about my parents I hadn't known. "But why, Hoyo," I asked, "why did you never tell us?"

"You know, Safia, that was our story; that was our pain. We wanted better for you. And, anyway, you children live a different life from us. Sometimes, we find it hard to talk to you, to understand this life you live. In Somalia, everything was simple: we all spoke the same language, believed the same things, had the same culture. Children did as their parents did: they did as they were told. Now, we live in Britain, Canada, America, Holland and we look at our children and we see strangers. We don't understand the ways of these countries; they are not our ways..."

"But we're the ones who have to live here, Hoyo. We're the ones who have to find who we are... if you don't try, you'll never understand what we are going through. It was easy for you in Somalia – everyone was doing what your parents expected you to do. Here it's different: everyone is doing exactly what your parents don't want you to do – and it's hard to be different all the time, it's hard to feel like you don't belong anywhere."

"But you know where you belong, Safia: here, with your family..."

"I used to know that..." I said, faltering, on the verge of tears again. "But since Abo's been here, I'm not so sure... I don't know anything for sure any more." Then I turned to her. "Why doesn't Abo talk to me, Hoyo? Why does he act like I don't exist?"

Hoyo took a deep breath. "It's hard for him too, *habibti*. He doesn't know how... you are so different from when you were a little baby. He doesn't know what to talk to you about... He's a Somali man, so he won't admit it but I know... I know how hard it is for him to be weak, to be unsure. But I'll speak to him, *insha Allah*, I'll speak to him about all this that you have told me."

"But, Hoyo, won't he be angry with me?"

"No, Safia, I know your father well, very well. He hasn't changed in all these years..." Her eyes went all misty then. "Do you know, through all those years, wherever he was, your father wrote me a line of poetry every night?"

Poetry? *Abo*? I stared at Hoyo. "Abo writes *poetry*, Hoyo?" I just couldn't believe it. That was the last thing I had expected to hear – that my father and I actually shared an interest, had something in common!

She smiled proudly. "*Haa*, your father was considered one of the finest Somali poets before the war. People used to come from all over to listen to his verses. That's where you get it from, *masha Allah*."

Then I remembered the rhythmic voices I had

144

heard at Awowo's place, the meetings with groups of other Somali men, Uncle Yusuf's comments – and I realised what it had all been about.

"But how come you never mentioned it? How come you didn't tell me?"

"I was going to tell you but so much happened before I got the chance: all the excitement, then Ahmed's disappearance, Habaryero's wedding, so much to think about... but I will speak to your father tonight, don't worry." She patted my hand and got up. "You're a special girl, Safia, don't ever forget that..."

"Oh I won't, Hoyo," I said, with feeling, "I won't."

I got up then to go and pray. When I prayed, I asked for forgiveness, for myself, Ahmed, Firdous and all of us. We all knew better. Now it was time for us to act like it.

***

Afterwards, I got my phone and sent Firdous a long text message.

Slmz, Firdous, hope u got home ok. Been doing a lot of thnkng about evrythng: who I am, wot I want, where Im going. Been a bit cnfsed lately but now thngs r clearer. I wont b c-ing fuad again or any othr guy. Its not rite – I thnk we both

145

no dat. I want bettr. I want more. And I thnk u do
2. I thnk u deserve bettr. U r a gr8 grl. U don't
need Amr or any1 else to make u feel special: u r
special. Just rememba dat. Anyway, mayb c u at
da aroos? Until then, take care plz. I will miss u.
Luv Safia. XXX

I read over it again before pressing the button to
send. A part of me felt glad to have 'ended' it with
Firdous. But I couldn't help thinking of her, alone in
that awful house with only Auntie Iman for company.
I knew now why she looked for love wherever she
could find it: she hadn't had it at home for so long. I
hoped that things would come right for her. I would
speak to Habaryero tomorrow – there had to be a way
to help her.

Then my phone rang and Hamida's number
flashed on the screen. I smiled and pressed the button
to answer.

"*Asalaamu alaikum*, you," she said, between chews
of gum.

"*Wa alaikum salaam*, you, what's up?"

"Nothing much. What happened at the movies?"

I heaved a huge sigh. "Long story, girl, I'll have to
tell you tomorrow, *insha Allah*."

"But are you OK?"

"Yeah, a lot better, *alhamdulillah*. What are you up to?"

"Just sitting here wondering what I'm going to wear to your Habaryero's wedding…"

"Oh, Hamida!" I cried. "Are you coming? For real?"

"Yeah," Hamida chuckled. "Mum couldn't believe that I actually wanted to attend a wedding so she agreed straight away. 'It's not an Asian wedding but at least it's a wedding!' she said. A step in the right direction, as far as she's concerned."

We both laughed and I felt a surge of relief. It was all so normal, just like the old days.

"So have you decided what you are going to wear?" I asked, remembering that I hadn't even thought about it myself.

"Well, I saw some wicked Asian trouser suits in Farzana's copy of Asian Bride – I think I might wear one of those. They really are quite funky…"

We chatted for a bit longer then said our *salaams*, agreeing that I would go to Green Street with her to choose her outfit.

***

After the *Isha* prayer, I heard Abo come home from the mosque. I heard Hoyo greet him at the door and start to prepare his food. There was silence after that and I wondered whether she was talking to him about

147

me, about what had happened today.

An hour later, I heard footsteps coming along the corridor towards my room. Then there was a knock at the door.

"Safia?" For the first time, I heard my father's voice outside my room.

"Abo?" I replied. "*Kaale…*"

And Abo opened the door and stepped in, ducking his head to avoid the low ceiling.

"*Asalaamu alaikum*, Safia," he smiled at me, his voice softer than I had ever heard it.

"Are you OK now?"

I nodded, swallowing hard.

"*Alhamdulillah*."

Then he looked around the room and a puzzled look came to his face. "What is all this?" he asked.

"Poetry," I said, simply.

"Your poems – or other people's?"

"Hmm, a bit of both…"

He laughed then. "*SubhanAllah*! Some girls have movie stars on their walls, you have poets! *Masha Allah*, that is good, very good." He nodded, sitting down on the other end of my bed, still looking around.

Then he spoke again:

"Hear me, poem.
Fertile mind,
Sing your lines,
Verse rise up,
Fluent words,
Don't run dry…"

"What's that?" I asked, curious, captivated by the delicate rhythm of the lines.

"You don't know who that is?" Abo's eyes were wide. "That is Gaarriye, one of our greatest Somali poets!" He shook his head. "It's true when they say that our youth don't know their own culture, their own history!"

"Well, Abo," I said slowly. "Maybe that's because we are waiting for you to teach us."

He looked at me then and I saw a glimmer of recognition in his eye, a spark of pride.

"*Haa,*" he said, nodding. "Spoken like a true poet's daughter."

I blushed then. *A true poet's daughter* – I had never been called that before! It made me feel special, part of something great and meaningful.

"*Haa,* I see that, in this country, Somalia means war, nothing else. But we have so much more to offer the world; we have our *deen,* our customs, our poetry, our art and, of course," he paused and looked at me, "your mother's famous *baaris iyo hilib*!"

He let out a great roar of laughter then and I laughed too, giddy with happiness. This was what I had wanted all along: a father, an Abo of my own.

"Ha, Safia," he continued, "I will teach you about our history, about our poets. If you want, I will even instruct you like my father instructed me. But our poetry is not like some of this mumbo jumbo: our poetry has rules, it takes discipline and precision – but I will only teach you if you want to learn."

"But of course, Abo," I cried. "Of course I want to learn!" I couldn't think of anything I would rather do.

Abo patted my arm and got up to go.

When he got to the door, he turned around. "But I don't teach for free, you know. You also have to do something for me."

"Huh?" I was puzzled. "What do you mean?"

"I am going to the local college tomorrow. I have decided to start taking some English classes and I need a clever girl to translate for me." Then he winked at me and smiled again. "Now, Ahmed and Abdullahi are back with some cakes. Hoyo has made some tea. Come down and eat with us."

"Yes, Abo," I replied, smiling, "I'm coming now."

★★★

That night, we all sat together, enjoying the cakes and Hoyo's sweet cardamom tea. Abdullahi had saved me my favourite pastry and he gave me a smile as he passed it to me. The conversation flowed in a mixture of Somali and English, everyone adding their own flavour to it.

That night, Ahmed told us some crazy stories that had us all in stitches and we all laughed together, for the first time since Abo had come home from Somalia. And I was happy, so happy, I could have cried. But I didn't. I had had enough of crying for one day.

That night, I fell asleep to the sound of poetry filling my ears. Shakespeare, Zephaniah, Plath, Wordsworth, Gaarriye, Angelou...

And then, just before I slipped into the darkness of sleep, came those eternal words of comfort: *bismillahir-rahmanir-raheem.*

In the name of Allah, the Most Beneficent, the Most Merciful.

***

As long as there is a dawn
There is another day.
As long as there is breath
There is hope.

Epilogue

Habaryero's wedding was great.

Hoyo worked like crazy to get the food ready and Abo, Ahmed and Abdullahi spent the day playing 'taxi' for relatives and friends from all over London.

I went with Hamida and Lisa. They got on really well and Hamida looked wicked in her trouser suit with the matching(!) shoes.

The whole family was there, the men in one room, the women in the other: Habaryero had insisted. Firdous was there too. She was really happy because she had moved back with Uncle Ismaeel and his family.

"Thanks for everything, girl," she had whispered as we embraced. "I owe you one, big time…"

I told her to forget about it. I hadn't told her about my conversation with Habaryero – I figured she didn't need to know that part. *Alhamdulillah* for everything, right?

Habaryero was late, as is the custom, but she was well worth waiting for. She looked absolutely stunning in her braided hair and flame-red *dira'*. The gold at her throat and around her wrists and finger gleamed and her smile dazzled as she greeted friends, family and well-wishers.

Hoyo and Ayeyo looked beautiful too, both of them wearing their wedding gold, their *dira*'s hitched up to show the *gogorat* underneath. Ayeyo led the way when it came time for the singing and dancing. And, when we all sang, "*Bismillah, sallallahu alaya hooyalay*" – in the name of Allah, may the blessings of Allah be on your mother – even Habaryero got up (which was not the custom) and had a go at dancing.

It was during a pause in the dancing that I got a chance to recite my poem. I had been preparing it for weeks and, now, it was finally time to share it with Habaryero and the rest of the family.

I had written it as a simple poem, from the heart.

> "*Sister of my mother*
> *Know this:*
> *In you, I have seen:*
> *Inspiration*
> *Sincerity*
> *Honesty*
> *Compassion*
> *Faith*

Love
Mercy
Combined
Enough to beautify all of womankind
May you have:
The skill of the nomads who carried the home
The strength of the mothers who fled the fire
The patience of the settlers on distant shores
The dignity of the survivors, looking to a new day.
Know this:
You are an inspiration
To this wanderer
Still finding her path
Still learning her lines
Still making her way
You were the one
Never turning away
Who spoke in the silence
Reaching out in the dark
Know this: I heard you
Know this: I felt you
Know this, sister of my mother
You are my beloved Habaryero
For now and always.
May Allah bless you.
Amen."

I recited with confidence, with gladness, a strange peace inside me. All the women were still, listening to the words and phrases of home, both old and new. Some were crying, others smiling. When I finished, they ululated loudly and started calling out prayers and greetings to the bride and her family.

Then it was time for the *buraambur*, the special dance that is always performed at weddings and, with a flurry of jewel-coloured *dira'*, the drumming and dancing began again. Hoyo and Habaryero came and hugged me, smiling, tears shining in their eyes while Hamida and Lisa pronounced the poem 'wicked'.

And as I watched Habaryero throw the veil over her head and dance into the centre of the circle, I felt my heart soar with happiness.

Alhamdulillah, there I was: a Muslim Somali-British girl, come home at last.

Glossary of words and phrases

Some of the words in this glossary have Arabic roots, and others are from Safia's Somali culture.

Abaaya/Abaayas a garment worn by Muslim women over their clothes

Abo father

Adhan the call to prayer, made before the five daily prayers

Ai hey

Ajanab/Ajanabi a non-Somali person

Alhamdulillah "all praise is for Allah."

Allahu akbar "Allah is the greatest."

Ameen amen

Anjero type of pancake eaten in East Africa

Aroos a wedding

Aroosa the bride

Ar-Rahman, Ar-Raheem "the Beneficent, the Merciful."

Asalaamu alaikum "peace be upon you."

'Asr the mid-afternoon prayer

Astaghfirullah "I seek Allah's forgiveness."

Awowo grandfather

Ayeyo grandmother

Baaris iyo hilib rice and meat

Baasto iyo hilib pasta and meat

Bismillah "In the name of Allah."

Bismillahir-rahmanir-raheem "In the name of Allah,
   the Benificent, the Merciful."

Bukhoor an aromatic wood, burned as incense

Buraambur a dance performed at weddings

Cadaan a white person

Daqaan culture

Deen religion or way of life

Dhikr remembrance of God

Dhilo a loose woman

dira' a traditional outfit worn by Somali women
   made from light caftan and worn with an underskirt

Duksi Qur'an school

'Eeb shame

Fajr the morning prayer, prayed before dawn

Gogorat an underskirt, worn with dira'

Haa yes

Habaryero a maternal aunt

Habibti "my beloved."

Haraam forbidden

Hijab Islamic headcovering

Hoyo mother

Insha Allah "as Allah wills."

Isdaya to leave each other alone

Isha the night prayer

Iskawaran "how's it going?" Used as a Somali greeting

Istinja cleansing after using the toilet

JazakAllahu khairah "may Allah reward you with good." Said in place of 'thank you'

Jilbabs an outergarment worn by Muslim women over their clothes

Kaale come

Kalab dog

Kohl antimony, used to line the eyes

Koofiyet a Muslim man's hat

Laakinse but

Maghrib sunset prayer

mahlabiyyah a fragrant oil used in henna preparation

Masha Allah "it is as God intended."

Midgaan the name of Somali outcasts

Nabat peace

Na'am yes

Nayaa hey

Niqaab Islamic face covering

Qaabil a tribe

Qaat a narcotic

Qahwa coffee

Raka'a a single unit of Muslim prayer

Sabr, sabr lahow be patient

Salaam peace

Salah prayer

Sheedh a traditional Somali woman's outfit, typically worn at home

Soogal come in

SubhanAllah "glorified be Allah."

suqaar a chopped meat dish

ukhti "my sister."

Wa alaikum salaam "and upon you be peace." Said in response to *Asalaamu alaikum*

Walaalo sister

Wallahi "I swear by Allah."

WarHassano a greeting after a long separation

Wudhu ritual cleansing before prayer

Xalaal/halal permissible to eat

Xalimos girls

Na'ima B Robert, born in Leeds and raised
in Zimbabwe, is descended from Scottish
Highlanders on her father's side and the Zulu
people on her mother's side. She went on to gain
a first-class degree from the University of London.
Having worked in marketing, the performing arts,
teaching and the travel and tourism industry, she now
has a wonderful time being a mum, running
a magazine and writing children's books. She divides
her time between Egypt and the UK.

Na'ima has been fascinated by Somali culture ever
since her first encounter with immigrant Somali
students in East London. The idea for
From Somali, with love came to her while
on a weekend retreat for Somali youth.
It is her first novel for teenagers.

To find out more about the author and her books,
visit www.nbrobert.com